AFTERNOON ABSENTEA

Baker's SurpRISE Mysteries

Book Two

R. A. Hutchins

Copyright © 2025 Rachel Anne Hutchins

All rights reserved.

The characters, locations and events portrayed in this story are wholly the product of the author's imagination. Any similarity to any persons, whether living or dead, is purely coincidental.

Cover Design by Molly Burton at Cozycoverdesigns.com

ISBN: 9798287073336

To Michael,
without whom none of this
would be possible
xxx

Books in this Series
The Baker's SurpRISE Mysteries

Footloose and Fancy Tea
Afternoon Absentea
Fake It Till You Cake It

Other Murder Mystery Titles by this Author:
Baker's Rise Mysteries -

Here Today, Scone Tomorrow
Pie Comes Before A Fall
Absence Makes the Heart Grow Fondant
Muffin Ventured, Muffin Gained
Out with the Old, In with the Choux
All's Fair in Loaf and War
A Walk In the Parkin
The Jam Before the Storm
Things Cannoli Get Better
A Stitch In Key Lime

The Lillymouth Mysteries Trilogy -

Fresh As a Daisy
No Shrinking Violet
Chin Up Buttercup

CONTENTS

Chapter One	1
Chapter Two	10
Chapter Three	19
Chapter Four	28
Chapter Five	36
Chapter Six	46
Chapter Seven	57
Chapter Eight	66
Chapter Nine	79
Chapter Ten	88
Chapter Eleven	100
Chapter Twelve	109
Chapter Thirteen	119
Chapter Fourteen	129
Chapter Fifteen	139
Chapter Sixteen	151
Chapter Seventeen	159
Chapter Eighteen	170
Chapter Nineteen	179
Chapter Twenty	189
Chapter Twenty-One	196
About The Author	201

CHAPTER ONE

If anyone could be called sunshine personified, it would be Sarah, Naomi mused as she hunkered down further into her cosy corner of the Three B's café, tuning out the howling November wind which had blown her here. Baby Rose, now a stout and inquisitive seven-month-old sat impatiently in a highchair next to her, hammering on the tray table with tiny, tightly clenched fists. Bored of the squishy fabric book she had been given to play with, that discarded item now lay forgotten on the floor, all of its corners soaked in baby dribble from where the teething infant had been sucking on it. Naomi had given up passing it back, and silently hoped Sarah would be finished with the bread orders before the baby's demands became any noisier. Sleep had eluded Naomi recently and her patience had apparently disappeared with it.

Unfazed by her own daughter's impatience, Sarah simply interrupted her happy humming to assure little Rose that her bottle and a biscuit were both coming, flashing a wide smile as she spoke that lit up her eyes in a way they had only been sparkling for the past couple of weeks. Naomi had no doubt that the fire reignited in her widowed friend's soul was from the time she had spent with a certain detective. Indeed, she was hoping to hear the latest instalment of their tentative romance this morning, before returning to Ginger's to complete her preparations for the afternoon tea dance taking place that afternoon.

"Still not sleeping?" Sarah asked gently as she passed Naomi the double shot hazelnut latte she'd requested.

"Not very well," Naomi met her friend's worried eyes and shrugged her shoulders.

"Have you worked out what's causing it?" Sarah took her seat beside them, immediately quietening the irritable baby with milk and a snack, "Is it just the general tension around the place?"

Naomi let out a small sigh of relief that calm had been restored, "Possibly, though now that Colin has taken the reins from Goldie and given us all detailed schedules and contracts that has eased somewhat. Maybe it's the shadow of the murder investigation still lingering? Or Tom stomping about the place like a bear with a sore head owing to an imminent visit from his father? I'm not sure." She stifled a yawn behind her hand and slowly spread raspberry jam on her slice of toasted sourdough, "But enough of that, how are things going with you and the charming Detective Timpson?"

Naomi caught the blush that spread across her friend's cheeks, even as Sarah made a point of fussing with Rose for a moment in an effort to hide that very reaction.

"Well, it's very early days, you know. We haven't discussed a relationship or anything, it's only been a few walks along the beach really, and a coffee up at the maritime centre."

"Mhm," Naomi smiled, sounding deliberately doubtful, "and the visits he makes to Bakerslea on every day off, just to sit in here and watch you work… Or in the Salty Sea Dog if you're doing the evening shift there. I've seen the way he looks at you."

"Shush! He's been a complete gentleman in every way. We're becoming good friends, that's all," Sarah couldn't help the wide smile that accompanied her words, any more than she could dull the sparkle in her eyes.

"If you say so," Naomi raised her eyebrows and matched her friend's smile, happy that at least one of them had something to give them that fuzzy warmth of nervous excitement.

She herself was feeling a bit jaded in that department, having finally accepted that she was attracted to her housemate, Tom, only for him to then pull away abruptly as the day of his father's visit loomed closer. All communication other than the briefest of necessary dialogue had ceased on his end, and Naomi had retreated into her shell, questioning her own actions and dissecting them in her head to work out if she had done something wrong. Of course, with the owner of Ginger's having inherited the building from Tom's grandfather, it was no wonder that a visit from that late man's son – the man who up until the marriage had been set to inherit the old place – would cause some tension. However, Goldie herself seemed unaffected, breezing about the place in her usual chaotic manner, flirting with the tea dance guests and arranging lessons with the two new dance tutors she had secured.

"Penny for them?" Sarah interrupted Naomi's train of thought.

"Not worth that much," Naomi joked, forcing a smile.

"Well, I do have another bit of news," Sarah handed baby Rose the fabric book as she lowered her voice, quickly eying the front door of the coffee shop to make sure no one was about to walk in.

Naomi's curiosity was piqued, "Oh?"

"Well, you know the way my Jamie was killed? By that drunk driver in a hit and run when he was driving back to us from Catterick Garrison… That they never found the coward who drove off and left him to die alone?"

Naomi nodded sombrely, wondering what was about to come next.

"Well... and I'm asking that you keep this to yourself. I haven't even told Kath yet, not until I have some information to share anyway, don't want to get her hopes up... I've hired a private investigator!" She rushed the last bit, breathless with the importance of what she was sharing.

"An investigator? Hasn't it been a few years though? Have they managed to find anything new?" Naomi failed to keep the sceptical tone from her voice.

"Not yet, not that I know of anyway, but he's asked to meet me here this afternoon so I'm hoping for some news. I gave him all the information the police told me after their investigation, about the scratches of green paint left on Jamie's blue Volvo from the impact, the fact the other car must've needed work done in a garage somewhere... He's been at it for a fortnight, so there's a chance." Hope bubbled up through Sarah's words.

"Do you think he can succeed where the police failed though?" Naomi knew as soon as the words were out that she'd been too blunt, and watched Sarah's face fall, "Sorry, sorry, I guess I'm just hoping he's not fleecing you, preying on your need for answers, that's all. There's a lot of conmen out there." Naomi knew she'd only dug the hole bigger, as a shuttered expression came over her friend's face.

"Well, I guess we won't know till I speak to him. Though I suppose there's a chance I've wasted my money and that's one of the reasons I haven't mentioned it to Timpson. I'm not sure he'd approve… though of course I don't need anyone's approval, and I didn't give the whole fee up front anyway. Only a fool would do that!"

The last was said with a defensive tone, prompting Naomi to reach across and rub her friend's arm apologetically.

"Well, fingers crossed. Please let me know what he says," Naomi said gently.

"Will do," Sarah replied quietly, sounding only slightly mollified.

CHAPTER TWO

Naomi was happy to hunker down in the kitchen preparing the bakes for the following day's afternoon teas, attempting to ignore the chaos that for some reason had filled Ginger's that afternoon. Even that refuge was not safe, however, as the door banged open just as she was reaching into the oven to take out her Victoria sponges, causing Naomi to shriek and jump backwards. The two cake tins in her hands wobbled precariously until she had them safely placed on the range top, as Reggie launched into the tirade that was admittedly similar to the one forming on Naomi's own lips.

"What the heck? The fool has arrived! Get out of it!" The parrot screeched, flapping his feathers at full span and looking ready to launch in the direction of the newcomer.

The little bird was particularly irritable at the moment, suffering from a case of unrequited lovesickness that not even the fattest blueberries could assuage. The housekeeper's parrot, Bonnie, treated her feathered admirer with all the disdain of a bird playing very hard to get, which had left poor Reggie 'all shook up' in the worst way for the past few weeks. To be honest, Naomi had generally had quite enough of his outbursts, though on this occasion she did agree it was warranted.

"Blimey, what's that?" The cause of the disruption asked, hovering in the doorway as he cautiously eyed the bird. The man was almost as wide as he was tall, his girth filling the frame as he mopped his sweating brow with a decidedly off-white cotton handkerchief.

Naomi tried, and pretty much failed, to force a note of civility to her tone. "Can I help you?"

"Aye love, it's thirsty work hauling pianos all day, so a pot of tea would be lovely." The bloke eyed the rows of cherry Bakewell slices on the countertop as he spoke.

"Those are for the guests," Naomi said bluntly, walking over to Reggie and calming his ruffled feathers with a practised hand, "and you're welcome to use the kettle if you wish, but I'm busy, as you can see."

"Not that jerk!" The parrot muttered under his breath, only slightly mollified by the slice of dried banana which Naomi produced from her apron pocket.

The piano man had now been joined by a much younger, lankier colleague, who appeared to be barely out of his teens and who hovered behind, looking hopefully over the older man's shoulder at the array of delicacies laid out in the kitchen.

"I think we've hit the jackpot here, Ernie," the young lad said.

Naomi was just formulating a swift, cutting remark that would hopefully get rid of the pair for good, when she heard the soft Welsh lilt of Carys' words from behind the pair.

"Our patisserie chef is very busy, as you can see," the housekeeper said, "but if you'd care to take a seat at one of the tables in the ballroom, where you just left the piano, I'll bring you some tea and biscuits through."

The petite woman attempted to bustle past the man apparently known as Ernie but, finding herself wedged between his ample girth and the doorframe, Carys quickly stepped back again and shooed the pair out of the doorway and down the corridor with a sweeping hand motion and several loud tuts of her tongue. Given no choice but to follow the Welshwoman's directions, the two men reluctantly retreated, much to Naomi's relief.

"Thank you, Carys. I fear my patience is as thin as Reggie's today."

"Not to worry, poppet. Cheeky pair they are. I'll get their refreshments before I go to clean Goldie's rooms. Goodness only knows why we need a grand piano when we have no one here who can play it and are barely keeping our heads above water as it is. Just an ostentatious waste of money, if you ask me. But mine is not to reason why…"

"And as we both know, there's no point in questioning it," Naomi added, moving to fill the kettle before remembering the four sponges still in the oven and rushing to rescue them.

"You're right there, petal, no point anyone questioning Lord Colin and his dictatorial decisions, eh?"

It was not the first time Carys had criticised the former gardener, who had now seemingly been self-promoted to Chief Operations Officer whilst the previously vibrant owner of the venue, Goldie, faded more and more into the background. The woman barely left her rooms these days, save for her dancing lessons with Carlos and Rosa, the new tutors whom Colin had hired. Indeed, the housekeeper's dissatisfaction with the current set-up had become increasingly vocal, to the point that Naomi was sure everyone at Ginger's must be aware of it.

"At least we get paid regularly now, and have set working hours," Naomi gave her standard response, annoyed with herself that she had set Carys off again on another of her moaning sessions.

"Hm, well, he'll get his comeuppance for ordering us around, I can feel it in my bones," Carys replied as she carefully placed four custard creams onto a plain white plate. "Best not be encouraging those blokes to hang around," she switched the topic smoothly as she made two mugs of the weakest tea with three sugars apiece.

Naomi managed a smile, though the tension didn't leave her body until the housekeeper had left the room. She knew well that Carys' real reason for her newfound dislike of their colleague was less about his decision-making and subsequent enforcement, but rather because he had refused the Welshwoman's request to adopt a kitten from the local shelter.

"This place is enough of a menagerie with those perishing parrots," Colin had declared, leaving Carys fuming. She had argued the point with him on several occasions, stating that the place itself was named after Goldie's cat, Ginger, so another feline would hardly make any difference. Colin had stood his ground, finally declaring that if Carys was to have another pet, then Bonnie would have to go.

The man might as well have said she'd have to donate an organ, so incensed was the housekeeper at his suggestion.

"That parrot is my support animal, my service bird if you will," Carys had shouted for all to hear, "and I cannot be parted from her!" It was the first time Naomi had ever heard her neighbour raise her voice, the woman's accent becoming thicker in her anger.

"Has it had training then? Been on one of those courses like proper assistance dogs?" Colin had continued baiting the woman. "I very much doubt it! Now, no more on the matter, I'll have no more animals in this place. It's like a zoo already!"

A bold, and decidedly misguided move it had turned out, as since then Naomi had noticed Carys' secret resistance to the man's seeming obstinance and power play. A spoonful of pepper in his tea here, a triple dose of salt in his scrambled eggs there… Small, petty acts for the time being, yet Naomi couldn't help but wonder where it would all end.

CHAPTER THREE

The following day dawned even greyer and drizzlier than the last, the weather not improving Naomi's mood in the least. Even Reggie seemed reluctant to leave the comfort of the pillow next to Naomi's to accompany her into the upstairs kitchen and living area in the room next door. The little bird smooshed his head further into the soft cushion and slowly turned his beak from side to side as if in silent refusal of Naomi's requests to shake a tail feather. With little patience of her own, she ended up scooping the parrot into both palms and hurrying from the room.

"Bad bird! Bad…" Reggie began, until that is he caught sight of Bonnie already on the fat wooden perch in the bay window, "Bon-Bon! My Bon-bon! You're my honey!" The parrot's whole demeanour changed as he took flight to join the grey bird on the other side of the room.

It was the same every morning, and Naomi felt sorry for her little friend, who was nothing if not a trier. Presumably, the whole scenario would play out as it usually did, with Reggie lavishing sweet words onto Bonnie, whilst she preened her feathers and made a show of ignoring him until their breakfast appeared. A silent truce would then play out as they shared their seeds and fruit, until the food had disappeared at which time the grey parrot would retreat immediately to her cage by the door.

Serving her feathered friends first before making herself a strong black coffee and putting some bread into the toaster, Naomi was suddenly struck by Carys' absence. Normally the housekeeper would be up already cooking sausages or bacon and eggs, the tantalising scents filling the whole room. Today, however, she was nowhere to be seen, and Naomi silently admitted to feeling rather relieved.

As she joined the parrots at the table in the window, however, Naomi noticed something much more worrying than her neighbour's absence. Indeed, in all the years she had known him, Naomi had never seen Reggie regulating his own intake of food – especially when said food was right there in front of him just waiting to be gobbled up. Yet, that was what was now happening, as Naomi studied the small, green bird. Very slowly, as if it were the last he would ever taste of its kind, Reggie was pulling apart a juicy green grape, all the while monitoring the object of his affections with a furtive side-eye to make sure she was still eating. Whether his intent was to give Bonnie the majority of the food, or to eke out their time together, Naomi wasn't sure. Certainly, altruism had never been in Reggie's repertoire before now! All she was certain of, was that her beloved parrot was both bright and astute, meaning it was quite possible he had cottoned on to the fact that Bonnie usually rushed away as soon as the feast was finished. Whilst sweet, this was actually a worrying development. For Reggie's pining and lovesickness to come between him and his food was a step too far, and Naomi knew she would need to think of a way to intervene.

Perhaps it would be a good idea to keep them apart for all meals? Naomi mused. *Or even try to limit any time together to the bare minimum?*

"No hot food?" Naomi had not heard Tom enter the room and so was surprised by the question.

"What? Oh, no it would appear not."

"No Carys today then? That's a first!" Tom filled the kettle and came to join her at the table while it boiled.

"Erm, haven't seen her," Naomi pulled her dressing gown closer and made a point of focusing on her coffee cup. When she had become so self-conscious around the man, she wasn't sure, but at a guess would say it had coincided with her realising she was actually attracted to him. Not that it was likely to go anywhere, what with her having sworn off relationships, and Tom being caught up in his own family issues at the moment. So, as was her way whenever things felt awkward, Naomi had been trying to ignore the problem as far as possible – which in this case had meant avoiding her neighbour altogether in recent weeks. With Tom away working whatever random hours were needed photographing crime scenes all around the region, their paths thankfully hadn't crossed too often anyway.

Until today.

"Unlike her to leave Bonnie out of the cage when she's not in the kitchen to keep an eye on her," Tom continued the conversation, unaware that Naomi was lost in her own thoughts.

"Huh?" Naomi dragged her eyes up to meet his.

"Carys. Unlike her not to be here at breakfast time," Tom looked worried, the lines of concern dragging his mouth down at the corners. "You okay, Naomi? We haven't had a catch up in a while. Probably my fault. Sorry. Had, er, a lot on my mind."

"I'm fine, and no need to apologize, we're both busy."

Tom looked like there was more – rather a lot more, in fact – that he wanted to say, but at that moment Carys bustled in, muttering to herself.

It took a moment for the Welshwoman to register their presence, as Naomi and Tom sat silently watching her as she opened and closed random cupboards in quick succession.

"Oh! I didn't see you both there!" Carys shoved the brown package which had hereto been clutched to her chest into the cupboard under the sink, which was the one that happened to be closest, and slammed it shut. A more furtive-looking person you would struggle to find.

"All okay?" Tom asked, his eyes flitting from the woman's face to the cupboard door, and back again.

"Of course! Now, breakfast for my lovelies," Carys took her apron from its hook on the back of the door, unusually fully dressed for this time of day, and studiously avoided eye contact with either of them whilst she tied it on. The strangely tense moment was only broken by Bonnie apparently having finished her food and taking flight to her owner's shoulder, whereupon the woman happily focussed all her attention on the bird.

Naomi and Tom shared a brief, eyebrows-raised look, before Reggie began his sorrowful lament at the sudden emptiness of the spot on the perch beside him.

"My Bon-Bon, she's a corker," he chirped at less than half his normal volume, eyes cast down to his clawed, scaly feet.

The pitiful tone tugged on Naomi's heartstrings, and she said a quick goodbye to her housemates, encouraging the sad parrot onto her arm and hurrying him from the room. The random package and Carys' strange behaviour instantly forgotten.

"I know, Reggie, I know, it's hard," Naomi whispered as they entered her own bedroom once more. "Mum and dad will be back soon, and then you can go home to Baker's Rise."

The thought of being without the little guy quickly brought a lump to her own throat, and Naomi forcibly blinked back the tears which threatened to fall. Being not-exactly-happy here herself was one thing, and Naomi had become used to the low-level anxiety which always sat deep in her stomach no matter her location, but seeing Reggie this defeated was a step too far. His little head tilted wistfully to one side, his tail feathers quite still and absent of their usual wriggling energy… no, this was a development in the wrong direction and something which Naomi needed to take care of right away.

CHAPTER FOUR

Despite the afternoon teas which needed to be arranged on their stands, and the lemon and poppy seed mini muffins which she was still to make for that day's dance, Naomi decided to sneak out of the manor house for an hour and head into town to buy Reggie some new toys and treats from the pet shop in the centre of Bakerslea-by-the-Sea. She dressed quickly in her work attire of black blouse and smart trousers before adding her black waterproof winter coat and placing her worryingly placid pet into his see-through carrier.

As was her habit nowadays, Naomi headed quietly down to the main ballroom and snuck out of the French door which was hidden behind a voluminous velvet curtain. This took her straight along the rear of the building on a path which bordered the back lawns, past the gardener's cottage where Colin lived, and then down through the overgrown and overhanging trees at the rear of the property to a small door hidden in the back wall. It was Tom who had originally shown her this exit which led straight onto the promenade. From there, turning one way took you up the hill to the maritime centre and the other to the town square.

This was a route which Naomi took several times a week. What was not usual, however, was to step out of the building and be able to hear a huge argument unfolding a little farther down the path, in what was strictly speaking the small private garden belonging to the cottage, but which was actually a borderless extension of the main lawns. Instinctively shrinking back against the manor house wall and pulling her hood tighter around her face, Naomi hoped her dark attire and the general gloom of the day would shroud her from view. To be honest, both men seemed so engrossed in their altercation that neither were likely to notice her anyway. Nevertheless, Naomi crept forward, grateful for a moment for Reggie's desolate mood as it meant the parrot was less likely to give one of his famously rude one-liners.

"…and I want to know what you're doing lurking in my bushes!" Colin bellowed as Naomi neared the pair.

Curiosity almost caused her to pause in her mission to reach the back gate, yet she pressed on slowly.

"As I've said, I know what you did! And it'll take a decent offer to tempt me to keep my mouth shut!" The other man shouted, just as Naomi reached the point where the path veered away from the wall and she would have to race along the remainder of it, making a run for the tree-lined cobbles that led down to the gate, thankfully hiding the path with their overgrown branches.

Naomi paused, her breath noisy in her ears as her fight or flight response kicked in and panic began to tighten her chest.

Just don't freeze, Naomi told herself, *either forward or back but don't freeze out here in the open.*

The noise of her own blood rushing in her ears drowned out the shouting accusations of both men, as Naomi's body lurched forward onto the exposed part of the old path. Luckily for her, their altercation broke into a fist fight at just that moment, and Naomi was able to hurry to the shelter of the overarching bushes without being seen.

"Murderer!"

The accusation rang out in the damp morning air, followed so swiftly by silence that Naomi couldn't even be sure that was what she had heard. Given the choice between returning to listen more or continuing on her way, she chose the latter.

Some things were best left alone.

Decidedly unsettled, with sweat soaking her hairline in the warm confines of her coat hood, Naomi took several deep breaths and hurried along the promenade towards the town square. To her left, the swollen tide was well in, the grey, foaming waves reaching almost to the pebbly edge of the beach in places. Naomi normally found the rhythmic motion of the water and familiar sounds of the coastal path relaxing, but today the whole place seemed to reflect her own miserable mood. The shrill tone of her mobile phone ringing in her pocket caught her off guard and Naomi fumbled to answer it, her heart beating nineteen to the dozen.

"Hello?"

"Naomi? Are you okay? You sound breathless," Sarah didn't sound too calm herself.

"Umhm, just, er, having one of those mornings."

"Oh, well, I don't want to bother y…"

"No, you're not, I'm actually on my way into town. Shall I pop in? I can be there in five minutes."

"Yes, yes, that'll be perfect, thank you," the relief in her friend's voice was palpable.

Naomi's anxiety ramped up a notch or three as she pressed on, shielding Reggie from the damp drizzle with her arm as she brought his carrier up to clutch it by her chest.

"Best bird," Naomi whispered, as much for her own reassurance as his.

"My No Me," the parrot whisper-chirped back, removing his head from the nestle of his inner-wing for only the briefest of moments to be heard.

Naomi wondered if she should mention the altercation to Sarah, or to Tom even when she returned to Ginger's. Then the thought crossed her mind that the man fighting with Colin could be Tom's own father and so she quickly decided against getting involved. The matter of the fair ownership of the manor house was not a discussion Naomi wished to be a part of, and from the change in Tom's demeanour whenever he mentioned the man, his dad was not someone to question.

Not for the first time, Naomi asked herself if she felt safe at Ginger's, then quickly changed the course of her thoughts before the answer could materialize.

Deep down, though, she knew the truth.

She was just one more incident away from packing her bags.

CHAPTER FIVE

The fairy-lit cosiness of the Three B's café was a welcome retreat from both the weather and her equally dreary thoughts. Naomi joined her friend at the corner table farthest from the door and slumped down onto her usual chair, careful to position Reggie's case on the cushioned bench next to her. The lack of welcoming hug was barely noticeable, given that Naomi immediately homed in on Sarah's swollen, watery eyes and her finger that tapped monotonously against the tabletop without missing a beat.

"Oh! I didn't notice you come in," Sarah shook off her heavy introspection with a visible wiggle of her shoulders, "I'll get the coffee on."

"It can wait a minute," Naomi replied gently, placing her hand onto Sarah's arm and rubbing her thumb lightly in reassuring circles. "You sounded stressed when you called?"

"I think I've made a terrible mistake," Sarah's bottom lip wobbled, and fresh tears streamed down her cheeks.

"I'm sure it's nothing that we can't sort between us, or with Kath's help. Detective Timpson, even, would always come if you asked him," Naomi rushed through the list of her friend's support network.

"I know, I know, I just feel so stupid, that's all. And it's not like you didn't warn me…"

"Start at the beginning," Naomi suggested gently.

"Well, you know I told you that I'd hired a private investigator to look into the hit and run?"

Naomi gave an encouraging nod, "Yes, did he contact you yesterday like he said he would?"

"He did, and I met with him at the back of the pub," Sarah dashed the back of her hand across her eyes, sniffing loudly. She took a couple of deep breaths before she was able to continue, "He told me he knows who did it! He knows who killed my Jamie!"

Naomi couldn't hide her surprise, "Oh! Wow, that wasn't what I expected you to say."

"I know, me neither. Apparently, he's traced the garage that the other driver used to have his car fixed."

"So, have you passed the information onto the police?" Naomi asked, the urgency in her tone causing the snoozing parrot next to her to wake and do a full body shake of his feathers.

"Pipe down!" Reggie ordered, before promptly hiding his head under his wing again.

"That's just it, he refused to give me the information without what he called an 'extra bonus payment.'" Sarah made air quotation marks with her fingers and lapsed into sobbing once more.

"You didn't pay him, did you? I mean, what proof do we have that he's actually found something?"

"Of course I didn't!" Sarah snapped, then caught herself. "Sorry, sorry. No, I used my paltry savings to hire him in the first place, I certainly can't afford more than we originally agreed as the balance."

"Well, at least you didn't give him it all up front."

"I know, but what if he does have that information? How could I not buy it from him? I need to get justice. Not just for Jamie, but for me, Rose and Kath too."

"I get that, really I do, but even just the fact that he's asking for extra suggests this guy isn't very scrupulous. What reason do you have to believe him?"

Sarah deliberately ignored the question and followed her own train of thought, "Maybe Kath could come up with the extra money? If I tell her about it all?"

"Um, perhaps, but is that wise?" Naomi was beginning to feel both decidedly out of her depth and in need of a caffeine pick-me-up.

"She's taken Rose to the soft play but when she comes to drop her off, I could…" Sarah had completely tuned Naomi out now.

I really could do with a more adultier adult to give advice right about now, Naomi thought to herself.

As if the universe had heard her plea, the door opened at that very moment and Detective Timpson stepped in, though his smile turned quickly to a frown when he saw Sarah sitting weeping in the corner.

"Sarah, love, what's happened?" The man made his way across to them in three long strides and hunkered down to be on eye level. "Sarah, sweetheart, what's going on?" His tone was soft and gentle, a far cry from the man Naomi had previously witnessed in full investigative mode.

"The fool has arrived! Secrets and lies!" The little bird beside them chimed in, though decidedly half-heartedly.

"Shhh," Naomi unzipped the carrier and stroked his downy head feathers softly, willing herself to blend into the background. Emotional scenes being really not her thing at all.

"Matt?" Sarah spoke confusedly, as if just seeing the man for the first time.

"Yes, I'm right here," the detective cupped her wet cheek with his palm, his soft smile crinkling the outer corners of his eyes.

Sarah leaned into his hand, her own tearful eyes imploring him to help her. When no further words came, Timpson leaned in and silently offered a hug, which was equally silently accepted. Sarah wrapped her arms around the man's neck and snuggled into him tightly.

Even if she hadn't before, Naomi now felt one hundred percent uncomfortable and took that as her cue to leave.

"Right, Reggie, we should be going," she addressed her comment to the little parrot as she zipped his case back up and put on her coat.

"Oh! You haven't even had a coffee," Sarah lifted her head suddenly from Timpson's shoulder.

"Not to worry, I need to head to the pet shop and then hurry back, so next time…" Naomi really wanted to ask if her friend was going to confide in the policeman but obviously now wasn't the moment for that.

"Make sure you look after her," Naomi blurted out instead, though her request was clearly redundant. She felt her cheeks burn red.

"Of course," Timpson replied, his smile reassuring.

Naomi noticed he was in everyday clothes and so must be off duty. The fact that the man must've travelled into Bakerslea just to see Sarah was very sweet and somehow made going back out into the autumnal weather seem even colder.

Reggie too was not keen to brave the elements again, and he let Naomi know it as she ran across the town square and down the main street beyond.

"Bad bird!" He squawked, "No bath time!"

"It's not a bath, silly, and you're a lot drier than I am," Naomi huffed as she pushed open the door to what had swiftly become Reggie's favourite place in town.

Assailed by the musty smell of animals and bedding, mixed with fish food and live reptiles, Reggie immediately changed his tune.

"My No Me! She's a corker! Ooh sexy beast!" The latter was aimed at the young female assistant, whom Reggie always tried to butter up to get a free taste test of their latest treats.

Naomi couldn't help but smile at his antics.

The forever antidote to her melancholy.

CHAPTER SIX

"Get the scones mixed, cheese, chive and bacon. Oh, fry up the bacon first. Have the scones in the oven while you slice the white chocolate and raspberry torte, don't forget the muffins…" Naomi spoke aloud to herself as she hurried back down the main stairs. Having dropped Reggie off in her bedroom with a full bowl of a new seed mix and a fresh wooden toy, she was finally free to get on with her actual job for the day, the afternoon teas. Her head wasn't exactly clear, though, hence the verbal reiteration of her to-do list.

"Carys! I wasn't expecting to see you in here at this time of day!" Naomi couldn't hide the surprise – nay, the pure shock from her voice as she opened the kitchen door to be met with what could only be described as culinary carnage.

"Oh, there you are, petal, I was wondering if I'd be filling these plate stands myself," the woman gave an unsettling giggle that came off more like a cackle as she pushed around a batch of half burnt Welsh cakes in a griddle pan on the hob.

The pan itself was smoking and Naomi worried that the wooden spatula her neighbour was using was about to catch fire, so gently took that from the woman's hand as she spoke.

"You've been, ah, cooking up a storm in here I see," Naomi forced a lightness to her tone, "let's just turn this burner off for a minute and…"

She was interrupted by a large ringing as the oven timer went off, causing Naomi to jump and Carys to shriek. Grabbing a pair of oven gloves, Naomi moved the griddle pan to the back of the stove, wafted some of the smoke away so she could see, and bent down to retrieve a strange looking bread from the oven.

"That'll be my bara brith, just like my mam used to make it," Carys' voice wobbled, "I didn't find the right ingredients, so I substituted some. That's okay, isn't it?"

For the first time since Naomi had entered the room the older woman looked unsure as she scanned the state of the kitchen. Cupboards and drawers stood open, their contents spilling out onto the old, tiled floor. The larder looked like it had been the subject of a raid and the fridge equally so.

"Of course, of course," Naomi reassured her as she checked the oven was off and then walked around slowly righting dishes and closing doors, wondering silently if her friend had truly had a breakdown.

"How about a pot of tea and some cake?" Naomi reverted to her true Baker's Rise roots, not for the first time thinking, *what would Granny Betty do?*

"That sounds lovely, lass, I'm fair parched. I'll get right…"

"No! No, no, let me. You sit at the table there and, ah, rest your feet," Naomi indicated the exact chair with her hand so that there could be no confusion in the woman's mind.

Thankfully, Carys followed the instruction, though not without trying to get up and potter round at least half a dozen times as Naomi prayed the kettle would boil faster.

"You'll have a cake, won't you? Like a flat scone it is, you'll love it. I can get us both one," Carys indicated the burnt offerings still smouldering in the pan, "really lovely, a taste of home, my Welsh roots, you understand? Now, don't be skimping on that milk…"

Naomi nodded, smiling, "Yes, I'd love to, maybe after this Victoria sponge," she placed two large slices on pretty china plates on the table, and hurried to add milk to the floral mugs, making sure to give Carys a double glug. "There now, all ready," she heaved a sigh of relief that the refreshments had been served without the housekeeper either causing herself any harm or creating any more mess.

"That looks grand, Naomi, thank you," the Welshwoman's hand shook as she lifted the cup to her mouth, only to almost spill the hot beverage over herself as the kitchen door burst open.

You've got to be kidding me, Naomi thought to herself, *I literally just got her settled.*

"Carys?" Colin boomed as he entered the room, "Where are you woman? You can't be hiding away just because you didn't get your way, there's jobs to be do…" The man's voice tapered off as he saw the two women sitting silently appraising him.

Naomi cast a quick glance at Carys, saw the older woman's eyes fill, and turned her attention back to their self-promoted boss.

"Morning Colin, we're just having a quick break. Which we're perfectly entitled to, I might add. You can see how busy we've been," she cast her hand out and did a non-specific waft of the room. "I can assure you everything will be ready for today's dance," Naomi forced a confidence she didn't feel.

"Yes, well, it had better be. Carys hasn't even got the tablecloths on yet…"

"It's all in order," Naomi ground out, holding Carys' hand in hers gently.

"Hmph," the man turned abruptly and stomped out, slamming the door behind him.

"What a… disagreeable man!" Naomi declared, filtering out the other descriptions she would have used in less delicate company. "I swear he gets worse by the day."

"Aye, he's a right one, to be sure," Carys sniffled, "he can't be giving orders though, not without getting his comeuppance. Mark my words, he'll get what he's due. I can feel it in my bones."

Naomi quirked an eyebrow but refrained from commenting, hiding her anxiety at the declaration behind a large gulp of hot tea.

They drank in silence, neither having the appetite for the cake, until Naomi's curiosity got the better of her and she plucked up the courage to ask, "So, ah, Colin refused a request again, did he?"

"That's putting it lightly," it was anger which underscored the older woman's tone now, not upset, as she launched into a lengthy and unnecessarily detailed description which meandered all over the place and made it hard for Naomi to follow.

The upshot was, though, that an employee from the local cat and dog shelter had arrived when Naomi was out to do a quick home review in advance of Carys adopting a kitten from them, and Colin had happened to spot their van outside and had stormed in and sent them away.

"But, ah, hadn't he already vetoed the adoption?" Naomi hesitated to ask, but wanted to get the facts clear in her own head.

Carys, however, simply employed selective hearing to ignore the question and ploughed on, "So, I went straight to Goldie, that I did. She's meant to be my friend, after all. Otherwise, what am I? Just some old skivvy?"

"And what did she say?" Naomi asked.

"She only went and refused to overrule him!" Carys, indignant and furious, flushed rosy all the way from her grey bun to her chest, "Said I'd have to take it up with the man himself!" She paused, picked up the plate of cake and slammed it back down on the wooden table. Simply to get the anger out of her system, Naomi presumed, as she watched a small chip of china fly off the edge of the vintage crockery and land on the tiles next to them.

Carys ignored Naomi's shocked intake of breath as she continued, "Which I plan to do, as soon as I've finished my baking in here!"

"Oh, er, I'm not sure that's such a good idea," Naomi ventured, meaning both the baking and confronting Colin.

"Well, lovey, don't you be worrying yourself," Carys' smile was eerily calm, as if she hadn't just smashed something in pure temper and for safety's sake, Naomi nodded in agreement.

"Well, why don't you get on with the ballroom and I'll make a start in here. Then maybe we could finish your baking, er… together and er… later," Naomi kept her tone deliberately soft but firm, hoping Carys wouldn't push back.

"I think I might have a long soak first," the Welshwoman said, as if middle of the day bubble baths were a habitual thing.

"Oh! Well of course." To be honest, Naomi was simply at the point of wanting the woman out of there so she could begin the big clean up that would need to happen before she could even begin her own jobs.

"Don't you let them grind you down," Carys added ominously as she left the room.

"Won't do," Naomi muttered after her, though inside her tummy rolled and her heart beat faster.

Once again, tension was building quickly in the old place, and Naomi certainly didn't want to be around when it all erupted.

CHAPTER SEVEN

The afternoon was waltzing its way to a peaceful conclusion. The afternoon teas had gone down a treat, the new dance tutors were a hit, and Goldie was presiding over it all like the Queen of Sheba herself, complete with Ginger Pawgers by her side on her own purple velvet cushion. There was no hint now of the owner's recent reticence or seclusion, and Naomi did wonder as she nipped in and out to refill teapots and collect empty cake stands if the woman was adept at acting whatever role was required to meet her own ends. Certainly, the way Goldie had flirted with every man there, jangling a cleavage enhancing necklace at one, and tilting a ruby-clad ear at the next was an Oscar-worthy performance given the fact the woman had lived like a hermit for the past few weeks, only emerging when absolutely necessary. If Colin felt his nose pushed out by their leader's sudden re-emergence, he didn't show it, simply fawning over her in a way that made Naomi decidedly nauseous.

The first hint that there was to be any drama other than whether Ginger would hiss and claw at another guest who happened to try to stroke her, was when Tom arrived suddenly, breathless and beetroot faced.

"Is he here yet?" He grabbed Naomi by the arm causing her to flinch. "Sorry, sorry," he quickly let go, "my father, is he here?"

"I haven't seen him," Naomi's tone was dismissive as she hurried away to take her laden tray back to the kitchen. Carys' bath had seemingly turned into an all-afternoon pamper session, and Naomi had been left to do everything alone, including setting up all the tables before the event. She was exhausted, and her patience dangled by a very thin thread.

Not that I would know him, even if I did see him, Naomi thought to herself, though that assertion was immediately disproved as a tall, broad man pushed past her just as she reached the kitchen door. Without a word of apology, he stalked down the corridor towards the ballroom, leaving Naomi staring at his retreating back.

That'll be him, then, she thought, telling herself to just ride it out in the kitchen.

Naomi's legs, however, appeared to have a mind of their own, as she dumped the tray by the sink and hurried back out to join the others in the ballroom where the fun had already started.

"...And don't think it's over just because the court ruled in your favour, I'll keep contesting that will as long as there's breath left in me," the man was shouting in Goldie's face, as the shocked onlookers sat mesmerized. The music had stopped, with even the piano player engrossed in the new entertainment, and the dancers paused where they were on the ballroom floor, as if in a childish game of musical statues.

"Now, I..." Colin tried to interject himself, though his small, rotund body was no match for the much taller aggressor.

"Get out of it, you little pillock," the newcomer snarled at him before turning his attention back to the woman garbed in jewels.

Naomi couldn't tell if this was the man she had heard arguing with Colin in the garden earlier, given she had been cocooned in her coat hood and so her vision was blinkered, not to mention her focus had been on evading discovery. Besides, the man had had his back to her. She presumed she would have noticed, though, if the morning's visitor had loomed over Colin the way this big bloke was doing now.

Dragging herself back to the drama at hand – which, to be honest, wasn't difficult, as it was almost like watching a live soap opera play out right in your front room – Naomi noted that even Tom was standing back, reluctant to get involved. Where before she might have moved closer and stood beside him, as a show of support, given his recent stand-offishness and bad mood, she chose to let the man face the music alone.

"You murdered my father, stole his assets under the false claim of inheritance and now you're here, enjoying the fruits of your illegal affairs. Well, it stops now, do you understand? This place is rightly mine, and I'd rather burn it to the ground than let you have it!" The man leaned right into Goldie's face, bits of spittle spraying over her.

"That is quite enough…" Colin began again, though it was the feisty feline who was to prove the star of the show.

Without any warning, Ginger sprang at the raging man, claws outstretched, and latched herself onto the top of his shirt with one pointed paw. With the other, she clawed at his neck, chin and cheek, quickly drawing blood as he fought to remove her.

"That's my baby, that's my little Ginger!" Goldie cheered the cat on, almost maniacally enthusiastic, as if this were some sort of medieval blood sport.

Naomi wanted to intervene. Certainly, she knew someone should, and evidently that thought crossed others' minds too, but not before the whole thing became quite awful. Several elderly men rushed forward, attempting to get between one howling beast and the other, and none came off unscathed.

Eventually, Tom left with his father, the man still threatening violence, and yet the place remained frozen, in silent, horror-struck awe at what had just occurred.

The moment was finally broken by Goldie, who began wailing and sobbing, prompting Colin to rush to her side and catch her just as the woman theatrically flopped in a dead faint in his arms. Staggering under the weight, the man commandeered some help to get Goldie to her chambers, though funnily enough none of the guests were keen to comply. Meanwhile, with barely a whisker out of place, Ginger sauntered after them, her head held high as if satisfied with a job well done.

I've never seen a more vicious cat, Naomi thought to herself, whilst recognising that was probably the last thing she should be taking away from the incident. After all, would she even be safe in her bed now, after the place had been threatened with arson?

"That'll be another three-day migraine, then," Naomi hadn't noticed Carys behind her until the Welshwoman came to stand by her side, complete with fluffy slippers, dressing gown, hairnet and rollers.

"Um, I guess so," Naomi whispered, suddenly feeling like her own legs might buckle.

"Can't say she didn't have it coming. That little showdown's been in the making for years," the Welshwoman added, her voice devoid of any sympathy. "Well, best get this place cleaned up."

As the guests filed out, some decidedly more the worse for wear than others owing to their heroic part in the proceedings, Naomi went onto autopilot to begin the mammoth clearing up job. It was her stock response in times of trauma, she knew. Retreat into herself, flip the numb switch, and don't allow herself to think.

She had an awful feeling though, that her normal self-help techniques wouldn't work in this case.

Was she about to have a front-row seat to the worst show in Northumberland?

CHAPTER EIGHT

It had felt like the longest day in history. Well, in her life, at least, as Naomi sat in her pyjamas, eating a Pot Noodle on her bed and enjoying the soothing chirps of the little parrot rubbing his head on her wrist.

"I know, Reggie, I know. Let's just stick it out till Flora and Adam are back from the book tour, then we'll head home to Baker's Rise for a bit." Right now, the thought of escaping this mess and going back to The Rise was a remarkably tempting one.

"My Flora," the bird squawked, "love you!"

"I know, me too, me too, I really miss her," Naomi replied, trying to swallow down the ball of emotion that had become lodged in her throat. She ditched the half-eaten pot of instant noodles on her bedside table and brought the snuggly parrot up to her face, letting him rub his wing against her cheek in a motion that reassured them both.

Reggie had been feeding off Naomi's own unsettled feelings all evening, and at this point their interactions were all co-regulation. The rain against the window was a constant thrum further emphasising the cosiness inside, and Naomi planned on an early night and hopefully a fresh, more positive outlook in the morning.

She was just drifting off to sleep when her phone began ringing and flashing Sarah's name.

Wondering what her friend was doing calling in the middle of the night and then realising it was actually barely eight thirty, Naomi's response was groggy.

"Sarah?"

"Naomi! Can you come outside, please? Round the back?"

"Um, yes, I suppose so, why?"

"Get out of it!" Reggie, cross at being woken up and then infuriated when Naomi moved him to stand up and put on her fleece jacket, made his feelings clear, "Pipe down!"

"I'm outside with Kath and… and I think she might kill Colin!"

"What?" Naomi was rushing from the room now, her mobile phone to her ear as she hurried down the stairs, the whole place eerily quiet since the earlier altercation.

"I'll tell you outside, hurry please."

"I will, but ah, if it's that serious maybe call the police? Or Timpson?"

"I called Matt, he's on his way but he's over by Ashington," the panic in Sarah's voice was clear.

"Okay, okay, I'm coming out the French doors now. Where are you?" The rain pelted Naomi in the face the moment she stepped outside, glad she'd left Reggie dozing upstairs.

Rushing towards the light that came from Colin's open cottage door, Naomi skidded to a halt as she faced the gardener who was embroiled in a standoff with Sarah's mother-in-law. Kath, holding what looked like the cast iron coal scoop from the open fireplace in the pub in one hand, and the long, spiked poker that normally lived beside it in the other, was advancing on the man in what could only be described as a semi-crouching, gladiatorial pose.

"We've got to stop her!" Sarah exclaimed, clutching Naomi's arm in desperation.

"Okay, okay," Naomi spoke loudly to be heard above the sounds of wind and rain, fat droplets dripping off her nose.

"Kath!" Sarah begged, "Kath, please! We can let the police sort it."

"What's this all about?" Colin bellowed, not venturing further than the doorstep.

"You fat murderer! You cold-hearted killer! You left my boy to die, you, you…" Kath's heaving sobs broke up her accusations, as she flailed the heavy weapons around in the air in a manner which completely belied their weight.

It must be all the adrenaline giving her strength, Naomi mused to herself, once again detaching from the situation.

"You killed our Jamie," Sarah continued where her mother-in-law had broken off, her own emotions rising quickly to the surface, "hit his car and didn't even stop when you ran him off the road into that tree! Coward!"

"And you have to pay!" Kath screamed and lunged forward, just as Timpson and his colleague Argyll appeared around the side of the main building. With barely a second to take in the whole situation, the detectives ran to intercept the attack.

"Armed and dangerous," Naomi heard Argyll say into her shoulder mounted radio.

"Mrs. Dawson!" Timpson shouted, getting Kath's attention, as Argyll rushed at Colin and barrelled him inside the cottage, slamming the door shut behind them and effectively saving him from being clobbered. It was clearly the safest way to diffuse the situation without tangling with Kath's makeshift weapons and Naomi was in awe of their quick thinking.

Despite the fact he was clearly working, Sarah rushed at the detective and clung to him, whilst Kath seemed to suddenly return from whatever rage-fuelled madness had been holding her captive. The older woman sank to her knees, the poker and miniature shovel suddenly too heavy for her wrists to hold, falling onto the wet path either side of her.

With Sarah wrapped in Timpson's arms, and him whispering reassurances into her drenched hair, Naomi crept forward and knelt down beside the broken woman in front of her. With all fight having left her, Kath was sobbing defeatedly in a way which broke

Naomi's heart to hear. Instinctively, and against her normal reflexive response, Naomi hugged the woman to her, unsure what else to do or say.

For the second time that day, Naomi offered tea, cake and a sympathetic ear in the manor house kitchen. Little Rose, who had been sleeping safely, warm and cocooned in her car seat in Sarah's locked Citroen, had now woken up and was enjoying Naomi's attention, being bounced as she was on her knee. Argyll had stayed with Colin whilst this cosier debrief occurred, persuaded by Timpson to call off the police backup for now, but Naomi was pretty sure a visit to the police station was in both Kath and Colin's near futures. In fact, she had no doubt that were it not for Sarah's personal connection with the detective, then this would have all been handled very differently indeed.

"So," Timpson said gently, his aloof, professional tone cast aside, "what happened this evening?"

He looked at Kath, though that woman had not spoken a single word since they'd been inside. Her hands trembled around her mug and her eyes were glazed over indicating her mind was definitely elsewhere. That just left Sarah who could explain what had brought them up to Ginger's. The notion of a confession seemed a bit absurd, since she was sitting holding the detective's hand, so Naomi judged this was to be a completely informal explanation that would be 'off the book' so to speak.

"Well, now don't be mad, love," Sarah began haltingly, "I wanted to tell you earlier, really I did, I just couldn't find a way to begin."

"I'm not mad, sweetheart, just worried about you," Timpson kissed her forehead softly.

"Okay then, er, well, I hired a private investigator to look into Jamie's death. He traced the damaged car from the accident back to a garage in Amble and got the name of the person who had the work done. I'm not sure if they hadn't bothered to give a false name in their drunken confusion, or if the garage just gave the investigator the number plate and he looked it up on the online MOT register or something. But, ah, basically, he found out the name then tried to get me to pay more for it."

"And you agreed?" Timpson asked. The man looked shocked, but to be fair his tone was still as gentle as before. It crossed Naomi's mind then that she was glad her friend had found such a level-headed man, especially given the hot-headedness of the ones she personally seemed to be currently surrounded by.

"No, not at all. I thought he was just playing me, so I refused. Unbeknownst to me, though, he then went to Kath in the pub tonight and made her the same offer," Sarah's eyes filled with tears once more and her voice wobbled.

"Kath knew you had hired him?"

"Not until then, no, but faced with the chance of finding out her Jamie's killer she must've coughed up the cash, because the next thing I know she's asking me why I kept it from her, telling me Colin Chillingham will pay, and hightailing it up here. I had to lock up and get little Rose safely strapped in, so by the time I followed her up in my car she'd already banged on the door for long enough to get Colin to answer it."

"I see," Timson took a deep, measured breath, though his gaze never left Sarah's and her hand remained firmly clasped in his, "I see."

"Do you understand? Why I did it, I mean?" Sarah asked, his answer clearly very important to her if the way she implored him with her eyes meant anything.

"I do, love, yes, I do. If cancer had been a person I think I'd have wanted to know their identity too, when it took a hold of my Evie. But do you not think if the whole thing was as simple as that, the police might've solved the case when it happened?"

"I know, I know, I have wondered that," Sarah scrubbed her spare hand across her face.

"I mean, could this investigator or whatever he calls himself just've picked a random name to give you and then fled with the cash? Or maybe he has a grudge against Colin and wants to implicate him?" The detective continued to be the voice of reason.

The idea triggered the memory of that morning, and Naomi told them of the brief fight she had witnessed between Colin and a man who could quite possibly be this private investigator, trying to blackmail the gardener into keeping him quiet.

"Oh goodness, what have I done?" Kath spoke up then, though it was more of a wail.

"Thankfully nothing permanent," Timpson reassured her, though the prominent worry lines on his forehead told another story.

Naomi nestled her face into the baby's soft hair and breathed in her newly-bathed, fresh scent, grateful that she had no idea what the adults were discussing.

If only life could remain as innocent as it was through a child's gaze.

CHAPTER NINE

The next day dawned both bright and dry which felt like a small miracle in Naomi's eyes, given that November in their corner of the world was normally bleak. The blue sky brought a spring to her step and a surge of optimism that did indeed feel like a fresh start. With no tea dance today and only a few hours of food preparation on her schedule for that afternoon, Naomi felt as free as a bird.

As a parrot, she thought happily as she watched Reggie hopping up and down along his perch, clearly also feeling brighter.

Avoiding the communal living room upstairs altogether, Naomi opted instead to get breakfast out for once. She had no desire to bump into any of her housemates and risk spoiling her good mood, though reason told her she'd not be able to avoid them for long.

"Ooh, sexy beast!" Reggie declared as Naomi opened a fresh packet of dried fruit and handed him a large, if dehydrated raspberry.

With her pet occupied she headed to the bathroom for a quick shower and then wrapped up warm knowing the blue skies were deceptive and in reality the temperature wasn't likely to have risen at all.

"Probably even colder without those rain clouds," Naomi spoke aloud to Reggie, who had red stained around his beak and was looking thoroughly pleased with himself.

"Rain!" He said happily, clearly having no idea what she meant but content to share the positive vibes that had been noticeably absent in recent days.

"Sun! Sun is better," Naomi smiled as he flew onto her shoulder.

"Sun!" The parrot agreed as Naomi rubbed her nose against his soft face feathers.

"Okay, I'll just be gone for an hour or so, and then you can help me tidy this room a bit," Naomi said.

Reggie scrunched his beak up at that, but her oft practised move had him in the cage before the little fella could say a word.

"Silly old trout!" Naomi heard as she left the room. The familiar moniker merely caused her to smile, knowing all would be forgiven when she returned with a bunch of bananas from the fruit shop.

Naomi was almost tempted to use the main front door, images of last night's showdown popping unwarranted into her mind's eye for a brief moment and causing her to question her usual route, but ultimately she decided to use the back path since it was unlikely she would run into anyone at this time of day. Goldie customarily slept till well past noon, and no doubt Colin would stay holed up in the cottage for a while, licking his perceived wounds.

Was he even taken in for questioning? Naomi didn't know, though she did recall Timpson saying there wasn't any evidence of anything until he personally spoke to both the garage involved and the dodgy private investigator. She pushed it from her mind, taking the stillness and silence in the old building as a sign that she was the only one up and about.

How wrong she was, though, as no sooner had Naomi stepped out of the patio doors at the back of the ballroom than she heard the familiar hum of the lawn mower. Without the cover of drizzle and gloom, there was nothing to hide her today and even had she wished to turn back it was too late as Colin had already spotted her.

"Good morning, Naomi," he shouted across cheerfully, pausing the machine and waving an arm in the air in greeting.

Whether it was safe to cut grass that was clearly soaked through to the roots Naomi wasn't sure, but it certainly wasn't a great indicator of a stable mindset, so she approached cautiously, only managing to raise her hand a few inches and flap it for a second.

"Beautiful day," Colin continued as she got closer, apprehension slowing Naomi's steps so that the whole thing was eked out further.

"Umhm," Naomi tried to plaster a smile on her face before she got close enough for the man to see her expression, her discomfort growing with every step.

"Still a bit chilly, though," he continued, apparently oblivious to her unease, or else deliberately ignoring it. "Off somewhere nice?"

Adept at picking up on tone and reading between the lines after a childhood mainly spent in foster homes, Naomi caught the new edge to the man's voice and came to a complete halt just before the path turned to head down to the tree covered cobbles. Colin stood straight ahead, mopping his brow with a blue handkerchief that co-ordinated perfectly with his light blue and turquoise striped tie. Why anyone would do gardening in a shirt, tie and waistcoat Naomi had no idea, but such was the randomness of her musings when she was put in a difficult spot.

"Just, ah, up to the maritime centre for a bite to eat," she lied. She was really planning to visit Sarah at the Three B's. Instinct told her to keep this information from the man, though.

"Really? I thought the coffee shop up there didn't open till eleven?" He left the lawn mower where it was and began walking towards her.

Whether it was the label of murderer still hanging over the man's head or some subconscious instinct propelling her forward, Naomi didn't have a chance to analyse as she broke out into a sudden run.

"Sorry, Colin, just remembered an appointment," she shouted back, slipping on the cobbles and reaching out to grasp the nearest branch to steady herself before she ended up flat on her bottom.

"See you when you get back then," the promise echoed in her ears as Naomi fought to unlatch the bottom gate and spilled out onto the promenade beyond, scaring a lone seagull that had been perched nearby.

When she was certain he wasn't following her, Naomi rested her back against the old stone wall that ran alongside the path, breathing heavily and feeling quite lightheaded. Of course, she couldn't blame the man for wanting to forget the previous day had happened, as she herself wanted to do the same, but something about Colin's ominous nonchalance had rattled her and Naomi was not keen to return to Ginger's any time soon. Certainly not without a friend by her side for support.

Cursing herself for leaving Reggie there, but too scared to go back for him right now, she hurried forward along the coastal path and fought to keep her tears at bay. She concentrated on the positive outcome of her journey, the destination, the goal, as a previous therapist had taught her as a method of at least controlling if not reducing her anxiety, and focused her mind's eye on the twinkling fairy lights that ran the length of the cosy café, the first taste of her hazelnut latte as it hit her taste buds, the smell of baking bread…

It wasn't until Naomi reached the door of the coffee shop and automatically pushed to open it, that she realised the Three B's was locked up. There was no light on inside and no Sarah visible through the side window as usual.

Naomi's stomach gave a somersault, and she clutched the window ledge for support as the panic attack took hold.

CHAPTER TEN

"Are you okay dear?" Naomi heard the words as if coming from a distance, from the far opening of a tunnel in which she was currently suffocating.

A small pressure on her elbow, the smell of dried lavender and still-damp wool reminiscent of Granny Hilda back in Baker's Rise, and Naomi's legs followed of their own accord as she was led across the main square and into the first building on the main street.

"There now, you just keep breathing and I'll put the kettle on," Naomi heard as she was helped into a low chair.

Sinking down into the well-used cushion, any springs long since broken, Naomi rested her head against the hard, high back and unclenched her fists.

"I'm not dying, I'm not dying," she repeated the words like a mantra, slowly controlling her breathing between each set.

"Of course you're not sweetie, you just need a sit down and a cuppa, then you'll be right as rain."

The reassuring words, the feel of someone stroking her hair slowly brought Naomi back to the present. A small woman, no taller than five feet, with kind rheumy eyes and long grey hair fashioned into a loose plait smiled down at her.

Now that the shock and panic had gone, and with it the fear she was having a heart attack even though she'd felt this way a million times before, inevitable tears followed, made worse this time by a sudden grief and longing for the women she herself had loved and lost.

"There dear, there there," the woman whispered, "better out than in."

Naomi let the tears flow, cathartic in their release, and managed a watery smile, "Thank you."

"Of course, now hot sweet tea and one of my homemade scones, that'll perk you up a treat. My name's Pearl by the way, what's yours?"

"Naomi, Naomi Bramble-Miller."

"Well, Naomi Bramble-Miller, I'm very pleased to meet you."

Before Naomi could reply, the woman had shuffled off towards the back of the room and for the first time Naomi had a proper look at her surroundings. Wooden shelves and pigeonholes lined the walls filled with every colour of wool and yarn, needles and hooks. Knitted jumpers and cardigans hung on hangers dotted around, mingling with baskets of crocheted blankets and files of patterns. A rainbow of organised chaos that reflected a lot of time and energy.

"My grannies would've loved this place," Naomi said as Pearl returned with a small tray.

"It's certainly helped me keep my head, my peace, numerous times over the years when life has tested me," the older woman fussed over Naomi, refusing to let her help with the refreshments as she laid them out on a high, round, walnut side table. "You stay there pet, you look like you've seen a ghost. Get some tea and jam into you, and the sugar'll perk you up proper like."

"Thank you, this is really kind," Naomi watched as Pearl added three spoonsful of sugar to her cup before pouring the tea from a china teapot that had certainly seen better days. She didn't mention that she normally skipped the sugar, accepting the wisdom that her body needed the energy hit. Besides, the way her stomach was now rumbling suggested any and all calories would be a good idea.

"I'm glad of the company," Pearl said, taking the chair at the other side of the small electric heater. "Now, if you need a listening ear, I'm happy to oblige, equally I could just drone on about my latest creations."

"I'd love to hear about them," Naomi smiled, grateful for the get out clause.

An hour later, with at least a pot of Yorkshire's finest sloshing about in her tummy and two scones added to the mix, Naomi left much lighter than when she had arrived. It had done her mind good to switch off for a while and her spirit even better to feel safe and looked after. She had even promised to bring Reggie to visit soon, after Pearl had mentioned that she had recently lost her own pet rabbit, Mischief. A new friend, a clear head and a warm sense of nostalgia that had somehow managed to replace her homesickness for Baker's Rise, and Naomi hurried along the main street to the Salty Sea Dog with renewed vigour.

The pub was quiet when she arrived, as it would be at this time of day before opening hours and Naomi half expected the front door to be locked. Relieved to find that wasn't the case, she poked her head inside hoping to spot Sarah without having to knock or shout. It wasn't either of the women who lived there that Naomi saw first, however, rather a somewhat dishevelled-looking Detective Timpson stood behind the bar, downing a mug of black coffee.

"Hello?" Naomi ventured further inside.

"We're closed," he replied brusquely, not bothering to look up.

"It's Naomi."

The man swivelled to face her, his expression softening, "Ah Naomi, sorry come in, I'll need another mug of this stuff before my brain kicks into gear."

"No worries, is Sarah around?"

"She is, she's just checking on Kath, be down in a minute." He refilled his mug from the percolator.

"Were they both okay… when you got back, I mean?" Naomi asked hesitantly.

Timpson came out from behind the bar and Naomi noticed he was wearing the same clothes as the night before, minus the tie.

"As well as can be expected. We gave Kath one of her prescription-strength sleeping tablets so hopefully she's managed to get some shut eye."

"No, ah, visit to the station?" Naomi's curiosity got the better of her.

Timpson gave her a side-eyed glance, presumably weighing up how much he should say before responding, "Naomi, I think it's best if what happened last night isn't made official. Not yet anyway, not until I've had a chance to do some digging of my own. No one was actually harmed, and I'll speak to Colin today and check he doesn't want to press charges. Given the allegations made against him, I'm sure he'll be happy to draw a line under the whole incident too. So, probably best not to mention it again, hey?"

Naomi felt the intensity of his gaze on her and nodded, "Yes, yes of course."

The tension of the moment was thankfully broken by Sarah running down the back stairs, her feet loud on the old steps, before she appeared behind the bar with Rose strapped in a carrier on her chest.

"She's gone!"

"What?" Timpson hurried to join her.

"Kath! She's not in her room, nor anywhere up there that I can see."

"Can't Dougal sniff her out?"

"No, he's gone too!" Sarah referred to their huge labradoodle, who had more energy than sense.

The detective's expression took a grim downturn, as he pursed his lips in thought. "Right then, we'll look for her," he declared, then paused and more softly said, "together, we'll go together in my car. I'll get

Rose's car seat out of yours and we'll go and find her together." He bent down and kissed Sarah and then Rose gently on their foreheads before turning to Naomi. "It might be best if you head back to Ginger's and hunker down for a few hours, we'll text you when we've found her."

Naomi was more than happy to follow the man's instructions, given that she was keen to avoid any and all drama like the plague right now.

Little Rose giggled and blew raspberries against her own hand, happily unaware of the stressful situation unfolding, as Sarah gave Naomi a quick hug and ushered her back out onto the street.

"The bananas!" Naomi spoke aloud to herself as she remembered the fruit she'd meant to buy. Distracted by this thought and envisioning the outburst she was about to face from Reggie when he discovered she hadn't brought him back any single treat, Naomi at first failed to notice the scene on her left as she emerged from the tree-lined part of the garden path.

All was quiet, no lawn mower, no arguing… too quiet, almost.

Suddenly remembering where she was, and annoyed that she hadn't waited beneath the shelter of the branches and peeped out to check if Colin was around before continuing up toward the main building, Naomi glanced quickly in the direction of his cottage.

When questioned later, she wouldn't be able to remember what her mind had latched onto first. Whether it was the perfectly positioned, small garden table complete with teapot and cups, nestled between two ornate metal chairs. Or the fact that Carys was collapsed on one of them, her limp body slumped over the table with one of the cups tipped on its side next to her. Perhaps, though, it hadn't been that at all. Maybe it was Colin whom Naomi had focused in on first, his body lying prostrate on the grass, his tie undone and askew across his strangled neck.

Either way, she would never forget the sound of her own screams as she ran towards the pair, the bananas long forgotten.

CHAPTER ELEVEN

"So, she isn't dead?" Naomi's voice wobbled as she clutched the mug of tea in her hands, "It wasn't poison as you initially thought?"

"No, lass, the medics think she just drank some sedative. Guessing it was in the teapot, laced in the tea, but I'll have to wait for results on that," Argyll sat on the opposite side of the huge kitchen table, swamped per usual in her massive overcoat. "It'll just be a wee stay for her in hospital."

"Just in hospital?" Naomi reiterated.

"Aye for now, till she's well enough to come to the station and answer a few questions. She's a wee bit groggy but no real harm done. Not to her, at least."

Naomi felt a whole-body shiver ripple through her at the memory of Colin's lifeless frame being loaded onto a stretcher.

"But why would she drink the tea herself if she knew she'd put sedative in it?" Naomi's brain fog felt like it was getting worse, "And why would she stick around to have a drink even, after she'd, she'd kil… done that to him? I mean, she'd been pretty mad at the man recently, but still…"

"Oh aye?" The detective's ears perked up, "Well those are the kinds of questions we'll be asking Mrs. Evans, but there's nothing for you to worry about." Argyll stood, causing Reggie to fly from Naomi's shoulder to the detective's arm, "Just stay here please and we'll be back later to go over your statement properly."

For some reason, which may or may not have been linked to the grapes she had produced from her pocket and shared with him, the green bird had taken a quick liking to the small Scottish woman. She, too, had a clear fondness for animals which obviously far outweighed her current job satisfaction, and Naomi wondered briefly why she hadn't gone into that field instead.

"Silly old trout!" Reggie chirped affectionately as he nuzzled around the wide collar of the detective's voluminous raincoat, probably in search of more hidden treats.

"Silly wee sardine!" Argyll replied, chuckling as she tickled Reggie under the chin.

"Silly wee sardine!" He parroted back, and Naomi just knew she'd be hearing that saying a lot from now on.

"Oh! What about Bonnie?" Naomi asked as Argyll was about to leave the room.

"Bonnie?"

"Yes, Carys' parrot."

"I didn't know she had a wee birdie too, but if you wouldn't mind looking after it till she returns... or at least until we know whether she'll be back here, then I'm sure the lady would be grateful."

"Silly wee sardine!" Reggie lamented as the detective left, returning to Naomi to recommence his nuzzling duties.

Voices out in the hall caught Naomi's attention just before a familiar face poked around the kitchen door.

"Sarah!" the relief she felt at seeing her friend broke through Naomi's shocked state.

"Is it okay if Rose and I hang out here for a little while? Matt needs to get caught up on the case. We came straight here when he heard."

"Of course. Did you find Kath?"

"No, no we didn't. We drove all round town, asked in shops, up at the old church and the maritime centre, no sign of her. Where can she be, Naomi? And why would she keep her phone switched off? What if she's hurt?"

"What does Timpson think?"

"Matt wasn't very verbal with his thoughts, to be honest, but judging by the look on his face he doesn't think her disappearance is a good sign. He went to phone her in as a missing person and get some colleagues out looking, then saw he had five missed calls, which even on his day off he's meant to answer apparently, since he's officially on call today, and now he might be in trouble for not being contactable and… Where can she be, Naomi? And what has she done?" The words had come out so fast that Sarah couldn't continue until she caught her breath.

The last question hung in the air between them, and both knew what Sarah was referring to. The women shared a meaningful, worry-filled look as Rose began to fuss and whinge.

"Baby bird!" Reggie squawked, fascinated by the squirming infant who had been released from the sling and was now grasping at her mother's chest.

"Is it okay if I feed her here?" Sarah asked.

"Of course, I think Tom must still be outside photographing the… the scene, and I haven't seen hide nor hair of Goldie. Argyll has spoken to her though, so at least we know she's not dead," Naomi clasped her hand to her mouth as the reality of what she'd just said struck her. The whole horror of the day hit her particularly hard in that moment, and she began shaking and sobbing.

"It's okay, it's okay," Sarah was there in an instant, her arm around Naomi's trembling shoulders as she crouched down, bouncing the baby on her knee with her other arm. "Why don't you come to the pub with me later? You could spend the night."

"Argyll said I have to stay here."

"Let me speak to Matt when he comes back in and we'll see what we can arrange," Sarah stood as Rose's cries became more urgent, "I'll feed Miss Rosie-Roo here and then we'll see where we're at with everything. Would you like to lie down?"

"No, no, I'd rather be here with you," Naomi sniffed and wiped her nose on her sleeve.

"My No Me!" Reggie chirped, waddling up and down on her other forearm, clearly worried.

"I'm fine," Naomi reassured him, bringing him up for a kiss, "nothing another pot of tea won't help, I'm sure. I think I'm going to turn into a teapot by the end of today!" Her weak attempt at humour did nothing to lift anyone's spirits and they fell into a morose silence, each with their own worries.

Naomi thought about Carys alone in the hospital, under police surveillance lest she try to leave. Then about Kath, wherever she had got to, a disappearance which must surely be even more concerning in light of recent events. And to Goldie, who had recently relied so heavily on Colin to run the business. Which brought her to Tom and his father, who certainly wished bad things on the place and its residents. Finally, she considered the young woman opposite, feeding her baby in a portrait of maternal calm and contentment. The man who was yesterday accused of killing her husband in a hit and run attack had just himself been murdered. Naomi wondered what to do with that thought, and what it might imply, but she dismissed it as quickly as it had arrived.

Sarah would never do something like that, would she?

CHAPTER TWELVE

Later that day, Naomi felt thoroughly guilty for even contemplating that Sarah could be anything other than a sweet and generous friend. Despite her own worry for her missing mother-in-law, and her resurfaced emotions surrounding her husband's death, she treated everyone at Ginger's with patience and kindness. Even Goldie, who had staggered in mid-afternoon, clearly already ten sheets to the wind, and had demanded a fry up. Feeling hungry themselves, Naomi and Sarah had cooked up some eggs and bacon for everyone, so it was a bustling kitchen table as Tom, Timpson and Argyll had also appreciated the sustenance. Goldie, of course, had disappeared back to her rooms the moment the demand was made, expecting to be waited on like the royalty she thought she was, and acting as if she'd barely shed a tear for poor Colin.

"She must be in denial, she can't really be that blasé, surely?" Sarah asked as she returned from delivering the meal.

"You'd be surprised," Argyll spoke around a mouthful of food, "we see all reactions in our line of work."

Sarah's eyebrows raised but she didn't get a chance to reply as at that moment the uniformed police officer assigned to the front of the house appeared in the doorway escorting none other than Kath and Dougal. Both appeared very muddy, and Kath had that same dirt seemingly mixed into the tear tracks which ran the lengths of her cheeks.

"Kath!" Sarah jumped up and rushed to hug her mother-in-law.

The older woman had a detached, wide-eyed expression, and her arms hung limply by her sides as she was embraced. She made no sound at all, which Naomi found quite unsettling.

Timpson rushed to get a bowl of water for the large labradoodle, whose tail no longer swished with his usual energetic fervour, whilst Naomi quickly refilled the kettle and set it to boil.

"Aw, who's this bonnie laddie?" Argyll knelt beside the gulping dog, seemingly not minding the flying water and debris that came off him when he did a full body shake right next to her. When she had covered him in strokes and hugs, the petite detective needed help getting back to her feet, given how her long coat had become pinned underneath her own knees. It would have been comical if not for the seriousness of the situation in general.

"Can you tell us what happened?" Timpson asked gently, once Kath was seated at the table with a blanket around her shoulders and a hot mug of tea in front of her.

"Happened?" She repeated, confusion etching her drawn features into even harsher angles.

"Where were you this morning?" Sarah tried.

"Oh, well I went to our Jamie's grave, just to talk to him," fat tears began rolling down the woman's cheeks.

"Is that how you got so muddy?" Timpson asked.

"Well, the ground was wet and slippery, and Dougal saw a rabbit and launched himself off after it. I was holding the lead, and, and…"

"And?" Naomi asked softly.

"I think I ended up in a grave!"

"A grave?" Argyll sounded horrified and Naomi watched the detective making the sign of the cross over her chest.

"A newly dug one, yes, and after that I can't remember."

"Oh Kath," Sarah stood and hugged her mother-in-law once again.

"Where was she found? In the cemetery?" Timpson asked the uniformed officer who had remained just inside the doorway."

"No boss, patrol picked her up on the road just near here."

Timpson shared a look with Argyll and frowned.

"How did you get out of the, the, ah, pit?" Argyll asked.

Kath stared at her with blank eyes until Sarah reiterated the question, "The grave, Kath, how did you climb out?"

"Dougal, I suppose he must've pulled me, I really don't remember," the woman replied, a slight defensiveness to her tone now that clearly wasn't lost on the two detectives.

"Hmm," was all Argyll said. She looked inquisitively at her colleague who was now scraping a hand across his face.

"There was that incident up here last night," Timpson said at length, sounding detached and professional, "we can't pretend it didn't happen. Not now that the man involved is deceased, a victim of murder no less. We avoided reporting it at the time, but now we're going to need to file an incident report, ask you a few questions, Kath…"

"Matt!" Sarah said, clearly feeling a certain betrayal on behalf of the woman she still comforted.

"Sorry, I, ah…" The detective clearly felt torn.

"I appreciate you're personally involved in this one, and I allowed you to persuade me to cancel the backup I'd called when we arrived here last night, so I'm not innocent in anything myself either…" Argyll's chair scraped on the tiles as she stood, looking first at Kath, then Sarah, and finally landing back on Timpson, "Perhaps we should talk outside?"

Timpson merely nodded at her and stood, hesitating for a moment as the other detective left the room, before whispering to Sarah, "I'm sorry love, it's my job, and now it's a murder case where she threatened the victim less than a day before his death and then disappeared the morning of the murder. Don't let Kath leave the room."

Sarah replied with a curt nod and turned her face away from him.

Naomi wondered what to say or do for the best and looked pointedly to Tom – who had been completely silent throughout, tapping away on his laptop – for a bit of support. None came, however, as the man simply took his plate to the sink and left without a word, stepping over the large labradoodle who lay exhausted on the cold floor.

"Maybe more tea? And something to eat for Kath?" Naomi suggested.

"I'm not sure how much more I can take!" Sarah exclaimed, her voice much louder than normal.

"Tea? Oh, I know…" Then Naomi realised what her friend had actually meant, "Sorry, sorry, it has all been a lot, and in such a short space of time. It's got us all reeling."

"I mean, should I take Kath to the hospital to get checked out? Should I contact my customers who'll be wondering where their sourdough loaves are? Should I try to get someone to open the pub?" Sarah looked to Naomi with wide eyes begging for guidance.

Naomi felt completely out of her depth and was grateful when little Rose, who had been having her afternoon nap in her pushchair, suddenly woke with a startled wail and made the decision for them.

"You feed her and sit with Kath, and I'll go and speak to the detectives about a plan of action," Naomi said, hoping she sounded surer than she felt, "at the very least we need to know who can leave here and who has to stay to be interviewed…"

Her whole body wanted to curl up in bed and nurse the anxiety which was giving her chest palpitations and sweaty palms. Nevertheless, Naomi pulled up her metaphorical big girl pants and left the safety of the kitchen, not exactly full of confidence.

CHAPTER THIRTEEN

"Compromised?" Naomi heard Timpson shout as she descended the thick concrete staircase at the front of the manor house.

Wondering if she should beat a hasty retreat rather than intrude on the current confrontation between the two detectives, she instead just froze to the spot, her nerves getting the better of her after all that'd happened the past few days.

"Aye, Matthew, what with you being the young lady's alibi for the time of the murder, your loyalties are clearly divided on this one, you know how these things work." Argyll spoke calmly, her hands shoved deeply in her pockets, "it's the boss's decision, don't shoot the messenger."

"I stayed the night at the pub to comfort her, nothing more. Sarah was understandably upset after potentially learning the identity of her husband's killer, and then watching Kath confront the man. Of course, I regret I didn't keep a closer eye on Kath too. I shouldn't have let her wander off unaccompanied in that frame of mind, we slept in by mistake, I…"

"I know, Matthew, I understand, and I'm not blaming you. I'm happy to see you in a relationship again after all that happe… well, it's a good thing, for you that is, but not for this investigation. You're too close, you know that. Your impartiality is compromised. And for what it's worth, you're not the only one with regrets about last night... Mr. Chillingham was fine when I left him, if a little shaken up, but he covered it with bluster and demanding we press charges. I told him to sleep on it, and said I'd call in today, then lo and behold he's offed before I can speak to him again. If word of that particular detail gets back to the office, it'll be both of us watching this one unfold from the sidelines."

Naomi heard Timpson's heavy sigh, felt the reluctance as he said, "I see. So, you're removing me from the case?"

"Aye, in an official capacity. You know I'll still keep you updated, and if you hear anything... Ah, Naomi how can we help you?" Argyll's tone changed to her professional voice.

"I was, um, just wondering if Kath should be checked over at the hospital maybe? It's just Sarah's feeling a bit overwhelmed I think, with ah, everything."

"I'm free to help her with whatever she needs," Timpson said, unable to keep the tinge of bitterness from his tone, "and yes, we'll get Kath checked over now that she's warmed up and had a drink, thanks Naomi."

Considering that her duty done, Naomi hurried back inside and forced herself to return to the kitchen rather than retreating upstairs.

"I think Timpson is going to come and help you take Kath to the hospital," Naomi still struggled to call the man by his first name. It felt too familiar, somehow, since she had first met him when she was just thirteen back in Baker's Rise.

"I wish I hadn't called him last night, then Kath wouldn't have had both of the detectives witness everything," Sarah whispered as she helped Naomi stack the dishwasher, whilst Kath played with her granddaughter. Sarah had helped her mother-in-law get cleaned up whilst Naomi was outside, though the woman's clothes still bore the evidence of her eventful morning.

"You really had no choice, I think," Naomi replied, "I mean, how would we have de-escalated it by ourselves, just you and me? Timpson's in a difficult position now, playing piggy in the middle. It can't be easy."

"I know, I know, and he only came rushing because it was me who asked him to. I'm just not thinking clearly either. And the guilt's eating away at me, Naomi, if I hadn't hired that fake investigator bloke in the first place, hadn't got him to open this whole can of worms… And where is he now? Scarpered with mine and Kath's money, that's where!"

"Of course you're not thinking clearly, and that's okay, very understandable in the circumstances," Naomi managed what she hoped was a reassuring smile. "Hopefully the police will find him and get you some proper answers. Until then, though, I doubt this place will be allowed to reopen for a while, so I can help out at the coffee shop if you'd like? I do have some experience in baking…" The last was said tongue in cheek and earned her a small smile.

"Really? That would be amazing, only if you're sure?" Sarah's eyes brightened with hope.

"Definitely, as long as I can bring Reggie… Oh! And Bonnie, until Carys gets home?"

"It's a deal!"

Naomi trudged upstairs half an hour later, keen to kick off her shoes and stretch out on her bed. Sarah, Rose, Timpson and Kath had headed off in the detective's car to the hospital and there had been no further sighting of Goldie, whilst Tom was presumably holed up in his room editing the photos from the morning's crime. Satisfied she wouldn't be disturbed until Argyll summoned her later for her statement, she let herself quietly into her bedroom and let out a small shriek at the sight that met her.

Everything from Reggie's large cage that was not either tied down or too big to fit through the metal door had been pulled out and scattered across the carpet and bed. Toys, seed and feathers were strewn everywhere, and to be honest it was the last thing she needed.

"Reginald parrot!" Naomi ground out.

The bird in question sat happily on his freestanding wooden perch, not even having the grace to look sheepish. Next to him, and so close that their feathers merged together, Bonnie looked equally unfazed.

"My Bon-Bon! Best bird!" Reggie tweeted happily, bobbing up and down on the spot.

"Well, I'm glad to see you've resolved your differences, but who's going to clean up this mess?" Naomi stood, hands on hips, staring at the pair. She had only left them upstairs together for a little while, not wanting Carys' parrot to be lonely on her own.

"She's a corker!" Reggie declared, lifting a wing for Bonnie to snuggle under.

Confronted with their apparent truce, Naomi couldn't stay mad at the two birds for long. With seed husks still stuck to his beak and face feathers, and his feathers all fluffed up to the max in pride, Reggie looked the happiest he had been in a while.

"Well, I'll just find a clean spot on my bed, close my eyes, and we'll deal with all this later…"

Spoke too soon, Naomi thought to herself as a heavy knock sounded on the bedroom door.

"Get out of it!" Reggie shrieked, clearly as unhappy as Naomi was to be disturbed right now, "Pipe down!"

"Shush shush," Naomi chided as she reluctantly made her way to see who it was. "Oh! Tom, how are you doing?"

Naomi could tell by the man's face that he wasn't happy, as he barged past her without being invited in.

"Not that jerk!" Reggie immediately picked up on the tension, causing Bonnie too to become anxious.

"No! No! No!" The African grey began shrieking, joining Reggie's tirade until Naomi could barely hear herself think.

Partly to get away from the racket and partly to be in a more neutral space, she suggested Tom follow her to the living room next door. Apparently almost out of patience, the man grumbled about the animals' smell, their volume and general presence as he followed Naomi into the kitchen area.

CHAPTER FOURTEEN

Naomi made her way to the small sofa at the side of the kitchen area, not wanting to get boxed in by the table in the bay window. Although he had stopped berating the birds, she could feel Tom stalking behind her, causing the hairs on her arms to bristle and her well-developed survival instincts to kick in. This, and the fact that she didn't intend it to be a long conversation, caused Naomi to remain standing as she turned to face him.

"I saw you," he began.

"When?"

"Out front, talking to the detectives."

"Oh, okay," Naomi had no idea why that fact would've angered him, given there had been another murder at the manor house that morning. It was obvious all the residents would be questioned.

"So?" He leaned in aggressively.

"So?" Naomi stepped back a pace.

"Why did you feel the need to tell them?"

"About Sarah feeling overwhelmed?" She was confused. Tom barely knew Sarah.

"No, stupid, about my dad!"

Naomi paused before answering. The man was clearly paranoid and very wound up. She needed to choose her words carefully.

What did I ever see in him? How did I not see beneath the oh so smooth veneer? The apple clearly didn't fall far from the tree... were the only things that filled her mind.

The delay angered him further, "Well?"

"Well what?" Naomi's own patience snapped then, the anger she had carried with her for most of her childhood rearing its ugly head as it had so often in the past when she felt backed into a corner. The anger masked the fear.

"If you're worried that I told them about your dad's threat to burn the place down, I didn't," Naomi was yelling now, "but if he wanted a private audience with Goldie, he shouldn't have made his threats in front of a ballroom of people! I haven't mentioned it, there's been too much else going on in case you haven't noticed, but I'm sure someone will. Not least Goldie herself! There's been another murder on her property so I'm sure she'll be keen to get the police's attention off herself."

Tom looked slightly taken aback by the outburst but stood his ground, "Her property? Her property? You do realise she sent my grandfather to an early grave and stole my family's inheritance? Her property? Pah!" He bellowed, barely taking a breath before adding, "And why is it that the killers always get the wrong victim?"

Naomi could only assume he referred to wishing Goldie had been in the killer's sights instead of Colin, and didn't dignify the question with a reply. She realised in that moment that in her haste to leave the bedroom she had assumed Tom would close that door behind him as he followed her out. That was clearly not the case, however, as a flurry of wings and feather entered the kitchen at that moment, swooping through the half-open door and diving at Tom.

Clearly alerted by the raised voices, it was a very angry Reggie and a slightly more reticent Bonnie who flew to Naomi's aid. Reggie aimed straight for Tom's head, whilst Bonnie flapped her outstretched wings in front of the man from a safer distance, whilst Tom could only bow his head under the onslaught.

"That's enough," Naomi said, "come here!"

Rearing up to leave one last, stinky message on Tom's head, Reggie appeared quite pleased with a job well done, coming to land on Naomi's arm with a flourish, whilst declaring the man a "Silly wee sardine," for final effect.

Seemingly unsure as to where to put herself next, and likely feeling the same fear in her tiny stomach that Naomi did in her own, Bonnie flew straight to the safety of her cage by the back wall. Seeing his love's retreat and that his owner was okay, Reggie left Naomi to join her there.

Tom wiped at his head with the sleeve of his jumper, "Agh, that's disgusting! If I had a shotgun right now…" He railed, his rage-filled eyes never leaving Naomi's as he tried to clean himself off.

A small drop of blood dripped down Tom's forehead, where Reggie must've caught him with a sharp talon, and Naomi found she had no sympathy for the man who had instigated the whole aggressive episode.

"Mark my words, those blinkin' birds are not staying! And you neither, if you've any sense," he added ominously, shaking a clenched fist at Naomi before turning on his heel and storming out.

Naomi's legs were suddenly shaky, her breath coming in short gasps as she sank down onto the worn-out settee.

"My No Me," Reggie joined her, and Bonnie too, perching one on each knee.

"I'm okay, I'm okay," Naomi said, though she honestly didn't believe it herself. In reality she was quite shaken and unsure what to do next.

Should she go and find Argyll, who was presumably still gathering evidence down by Colin's cottage, and report Tom's ambiguous threats? Should she try to talk to Goldie, who was probably still either drunk or hungover by now despite it only being late afternoon? Or secret option C, should she pack a bag for her and another for the birds and high tail it down to the town centre to wait for Sarah and Timpson to get back?

Not convinced that she could cope with another heated conversation, either with Tom or her employer, Naomi opted for the latter, forcing her jelly-like legs back into a standing position and causing the two parrots to move to her shoulders instead.

"Best birds," Naomi whispered praise as she stuck her head out of the room to check the coast was clear and then hurried into her bedroom next door.

"Best birds," Reggie echoed happily. The parrot had clearly forgotten the mess he and Bonnie had created earlier in the bedroom, and he landed on the bed now with greedy eyes, as if someone had laid out a seeded feast just for him as a reward for his efforts!

Leaving the two guzzling parrots to it, Naomi collected up as many of her belongings as she could fit into her holdall and then collapsed Reggie's travel perch to take with her. She hoped that with their newfound affection the two birds would be happy to share Reggie's carry case for the short trip.

The last thing to do, and the task for which Naomi had the least appetite right now, was to make a quick foray back into the kitchen to try to find the bag of Bonnie's particular brand of birdseed which Carys kept there. Naomi contemplated just buying some in the pet shop, but it would hopefully be a simple, two-minute dash there and back so she decided to brave it, presuming Tom would be licking his wounds elsewhere for the next while.

Not finding the seed beside or behind Bonnie's cage, Naomi started opening the kitchen cupboards in a frantic race against her anxiety's internal clock. Coming to the cupboard under the sink, she spotted the food bag immediately, but not before a brown paper package fell out onto her toes.

The one Carys was hiding the other morning! Naomi remembered.

Just as she bent further to retrieve the package, the door to the room squeaked and she felt someone's presence in the doorway, their eyes upon her. Naomi had no choice but to turn and face them.

CHAPTER FIFTEEN

"It's just me," Argyll said as she clocked Naomi's panicked expression.

"Detective, you're a welcome sight," Naomi breathed a deep sigh of relief, belatedly realising that she was clutching the secret package to her chest, its contents as yet unknown.

"What's that you've got there?" Argyll asked, noticing the direction of Naomi's gaze.

"I'm not actually sure, it just fell out of the cupboard while I was looking for Bonnie's parrot seed," Naomi realised the excuse sounded feeble, and hoped to goodness there was nothing incriminating inside.

"It doesn't belong to you?" The detective asked, joining her by the sink.

"No, I, ah, saw Carys putting it in here the other morning and thought nothing more of it till now."

"Well, since the lady in question isn't here, we might as well…" Argyll took the parcel and pulled it open at one end.

For a small woman, she's got a lot of strength in those hands, Naomi thought randomly as she watched the brown covering split open to reveal clear bubble wrap beneath.

"Right, what have we got here?" Argyll wondered, as Naomi prayed it was nothing that would incriminate Carys further.

Please don't be poison, or a weapon, or the sedative… Naomi thought to herself. She didn't want to be responsible for getting the housekeeper in further trouble and opening herself up to another tongue-lashing from anyone.

The plastic wrap was even harder to get through, but the detective managed without the need for scissors, and Naomi watched with bated breath as several bright, shiny objects fell out onto the worktop, accompanied by the tinkling sound of small bells and the odd squeak or two.

"Cat toys!" she exclaimed happily, relief flooding her.

"Does the lady have a cat? I thought it was just the wee parrot that needed taken care of. I don't want to leave any animal struggling without while Mrs. Evans is incapacitated," Argyll said.

"No, no, but she was hoping to get one from the local rescue…" Naomi began as the detective indicated they should take a seat at the table.

No sooner had Naomi begun the explanation than she regretted starting it. Obviously, to mention Carys' desire for a new feline companion inevitably led to her having to describe what – or rather who – had put their foot down about it.

"So, the deceased Mr. Chillingham refused her request?" The detective leaned in, ears pricked for information pertinent to the murder case.

"Um, ah, well yes. He had said no, but Carys must've gone about arranging the adoption anyway behind his back, hence her hiding the new toys."

"And that was that?" Argyll asked.

Naomi hesitated, and the detective was onto the pause like Reggie pouncing on blueberries.

"There was something else," Argyll said astutely.

"Um, well, yes. It's just that yesterday I went into town and when I came back Carys was acting a bit unhinged… very distressed, I mean."

"Did she say why?" Argyll had her notebook and pen out now and was jotting everything down.

"Not at first, but then Colin came in and I learned he'd sent away the person from the animal rescue who had come to do the home check ahead of the adoption. Clearly, that's what had made Carys so mad."

"Had he now?" Argyll's eyes gleamed, "Now, what kind of man would stand in the way of a wee kitty finding their forever home? No wonder Mrs. Evans was mad. Angry enough to kill, do you reckon?"

Naomi was caught off guard by the probing question and spoke without thinking, "Possibly."

"Indeed," Argyll tapped her pencil off the table a couple of times, her eyes scrunched in thought. "Now, the china tea set that was laid out outside, was that there when you left this morning?"

"What? Oh, no, nor the table and chairs. Colin was mowing the lawn when I passed by."

"A strange thing to be doing after so much rain, don't you think?" The detective asked.

"I did think that, actually," Naomi wasn't sure what she should and shouldn't say any more, so decided to stick with the truth, knowing she'd probably already said too much anyway.

"Especially after being threatened and almost physically assaulted on his own doorstep the night before, you'd think he'd want a lie in and time to lick his wounds so to speak."

"I guess so."

"Did he speak to you at all?" Argyll continued.

"He, um, said good morning, just pleasantries, I think. I was in a hurry to get away to be honest. After everything Kath accused him of the night before…"

"Quite so, and who do you think he was cutting the grass to impress? Is that particular crockery used for the afternoon dances, or do you think it belonged to the deceased?"

"I haven't seen it before, so I guess it was Colin's own, I'm not sure." Naomi's forehead wrinkled as her mind became cluttered with information.

"So, if we assume the deceased set up the little tea for two, then should we assume he added the sedative to the teapot himself? Was he trying to drug someone and it turned ugly before he could?" The detective mused out loud.

"Or the murderer could've brought it and added the medication when he had his back turned?" Naomi clasped her hand to her mouth, shocked that she might have dropped anyone in it.

"Hmm, yes indeed, very interesting," Argyll continued to scribble. "It would have to be a powerful person to overcome such a stout man, and to strangle him to unconsciousness, let alone death. But then Mrs. Dawson did demonstrate for us last night how adrenaline can help us achieve the unexpected in that sense."

Keen to get the spotlight off Kath, Naomi blurted, "Has Carys said how she came to drink the sedative?"

"Mrs. Evans? The detective who interviewed her a short while ago at the hospital has noted she said that…" Argyll flipped back a couple of pages in her notebook and quoted, "said that 'upon discovering the lifeless body, I sank down on the chair and poured a cup of tea to steady my nerves. Had I not lost consciousness of course I would have gone back into the house to call the police.'"

"So, she discovered the body? Poor Carys," Naomi said.

"Apparently so," the detective didn't sound convinced, "we're taking her to the station later for a proper statement, so I'll withhold judgment for now. There's a lot of moving parts – or rather, people, here, aren't there Naomi?"

"I guess so."

"A lot of particularly unstable personalities centred around this place, it would seem. Can you think of any more to add to the list?"

Naomi's mind went immediately to Tom and his insistence that she not tell the police about his father's outburst. Her head told her to confide in Argyll, but her anxiety at the thought of the photographer's reaction if she did… well, the latter won out and Naomi simply shook her head silently.

"That's a lot for now, it's been a stressful day," Argyll stood, struggling to find her inside pocket to return her notebook and pen.

"If I stay in town, at the pub with Sarah, will that be okay?" It came out in a rush.

"Aye lass, that'll be fine," the detective smiled and left the room as quietly as she had arrived, leaving Naomi to swallow down the nausea that rose up suddenly.

She had the sinking feeling that either Carys or Kath was going to turn out to be a killer, since the evidence clearly led to those two, but Naomi fervently wished that were not the case.

What she was certain of, though, was that the fallout from this latest crime was going to mean huge changes both at Ginger's and for poor Sarah and Rose at the Salty Sea Dog.

Changes none of them had any control over.

CHAPTER SIXTEEN

After spending a mostly quiet night at the Salty Sea Dog, where Sarah had kindly given her a cosy en suite room, complete with king sized bed and a mini fridge left over from when Kath used to run the upstairs of the pub as Bed and Breakfast accommodation, Naomi left with both parrots to go and open up the Three B's café. Having worked at the Tearoom on the Rise back home for many years, she was quite well prepared to make hot drinks and serve customers, whilst her patisserie training would hopefully come in handy to keep the bakery customers happy.

Sarah looked exhausted as she waved Naomi goodbye with a wriggling baby in her arms and a lazy labradoodle lolling by her feet. After having Kath checked at the hospital yesterday, where thankfully only a few minor cuts and bruises were found, Argyll had asked Timpson to bring her down to the police station for questioning. It wasn't until almost eleven at night that the poor woman was dropped back at the pub by a police patrol car, and Naomi had heard her crying as Sarah and Timpson had tried to comfort her in the next room. Presumably a sleeping tablet mixed with sheer exhaustion had done the trick, as by midnight the place had settled into silence. The pub would remain closed for the next few days, which Naomi hoped would give both Sarah and Kath a chance to rest and recover.

Such an awful situation, which made Naomi's heart and feet heavy as she walked up the main street towards the town square. Of course, Bakerslea-by-the Sea was abuzz with gossip that there'd been another murder up at the manor house, and Naomi received a few pointed looks and whispers as she made her way up the road. She kept her head down, her eyes focused on the bird carrier in her hand where Reggie and Bonnie chirped away in bonded contentment.

"Naomi!" A muffled call through the glass beside her caught Naomi's attention and she looked up to see Pearl waving at her from between two tall wool displays.

Following the older woman's beckoning, Naomi went into the little shop to be struck immediately by the smell of coffee and baking. Having not wanted to give Sarah anything else to do, Naomi had avoided the kitchen at the pub, and so her stomach rumbled now at the thought of breakfast.

"Have you eaten, pet?" Pearl asked, looking hopeful for some company.

"I haven't, and I have a few minutes before I need to open the coffee shop," Naomi smiled widely.

"Well, that's just perfect, get yourself sat down, I've got pains au chocolat in the oven and I've just ground some fresh coffee beans."

"You have no idea how good that sounds," Naomi sat once more in the sinking, highbacked armchair and placed her feathered charges gently on the floor.

"She's a corker!" The little voice carried up to them.

"And who do we have here?" Pearl asked, bending as far as she could, which admittedly was nowhere near low enough to see into the case.

Naomi lifted the carrier onto her knees to give her new friend a better look.

"You sexy beast!" Reggie declared, peering up at the woman whose grey hair was today tied up in a messy bun, complete with purple velvet bow.

"Ooh, he's a cheeky chap!" Pearl declared, delighted. "You're a cheeky Charlie, aren't you?"

"Cheeky Charlie," Reggie parroted back, whilst Bonnie, still unsure of strangers, stuck to his side like glue.

"He certainly is," Naomi agreed, "Pearl, please meet Reggie and Bonnie. I'm just birdsitting Bonnie while her mum is, ah, not available."

Pearl gave a knowing nod, "I've heard, yes, more drama up at the old Hadley place. They really should've knocked that house down long ago, not give planning permission for it to be renovated." She disappeared behind Naomi to prepare the drinks.

"The worst kind of drama," Naomi said, raising her voice slightly to be heard above the coffee machine and remembering that's how the locals referred to Ginger's, "I'm just having a breather from it."

"Good for you too, sweetie," Pearl said as she bustled about in the tiny kitchenette that hid behind a faded floral curtain to the rear.

Ten minutes later, cosied up with the warm pastries, and with the bird carrier unzipped so that the parrots could enjoy some slices of apple and banana which Pearl had provided, and which had made her an instant hit, Naomi felt her body finally begin to relax fully. She hadn't even been aware she'd been holding so much tension, until she felt her shoulders were no longer stuck up near her chin, and she could breathe in and out fully without her heart racing.

"You haven't been in Bakerslea for long?" Pearl asked.

"No, just a few months. I was hoping it would be a fresh start in a new place, but it hasn't quite worked out that way."

"Sometimes we think we need a brand-new location, new job, new everything," Pearl said, her old eyes smiling, "when what we really need is just a fresh challenge in a place we're familiar with."

The simplicity and magnitude of that statement hit Naomi in a way that meant she could only nod.

How different would things be right now, she wondered, *if I'd gone home to Baker's Rise instead of taking the job at Ginger's?*

It was hardly the grand patisserie cheffing opportunity she'd hoped for, nor had it come with the sense of accomplishment and independence Naomi had sought.

"I tried it once, the travel malarky," Pearl filled in what could have become an awkward silence, "after my Norman died. I thought I couldn't bear to be here in Bakerslea without him, thought I should branch out and make a new life on my own. Got as far as a caravan in Hove before I realised that all the beautiful scenery, all the new experiences in the world couldn't make me happy the way being here at home always does. Thankfully I had only rented this place out, so I moved into the flat above as I'd sold our family house to have my fresh start. Guess I'm just a homebody at heart. I need the support network of friends I have here, my crafting groups and tea mornings up at the church, and I like my grandchildren to know where they can find me for sweets and biscuits!"

Naomi nodded, trying not to let the tears spill over. She had a place like that, too. A place she felt happy and safe. A place people knew her and where there'd always be a whole community on hand to help out if needed. And she wanted it back.

CHAPTER SEVENTEEN

"And just remember, there's no shame in admitting we've made a mistake," Pearl clutched Naomi to her in a tight hug, "and my door is always open – to you and those cheeky parrots!"

"Thank you," Naomi held back the emotion that threatened to overwhelm her, aware she still had a job to do at Three B's, "I will."

"Best bird!" Reggie gave his own parting shot as they walked away.

Following Sarah's earlier instructions, Naomi located the switch to turn on the fairy lights, immediately making the small café seem much warmer. She walked around starting up the coffee machine and setting the oven to warm up, familiarising herself with the location of everything she would need before flipping the sign on the door to 'Open'.

With Reggie used to having free rein in the tearoom back in Baker's Rise, and knowing she couldn't keep them cooped up in the carrier all day, Naomi let the parrots out and made it clear they were only to use the wooden back of one of the chairs as a perch. She laid a black bin bag underneath to catch any little parcels and positioned a water bowl on the seat itself.

"Now, you've had two breakfasts already, so no more snacking till at least eleven o'clock!" Naomi's words, which she knew Reggie would understand the gist of if not the entire sentence, earned her no response other than a glowering side eye from the green feathered glutton.

"Probably talking to myself then," Naomi said aloud, as a familiar figure out in the square caught her eye.

Trying to peer out the window, whilst also keeping herself hidden from view was not an easy feat, Naomi found, as she watched the man in question pause to sit on one of the wrought iron benches that formed a quad shape in the middle of the town square. Within minutes he had been joined by his son, none other than Tom Hornsley, and Naomi shrank back further in case she was spotted. Unlikely at this distance, but after witnessing the temper that was clearly shared by the men in that family, she had no wish to trigger another confrontation.

Looking around rather furtively, the elder Hornsley reached beneath the bench and recovered a worn, tan leather holdall, which he then shoved onto Tom's lap. A brief set of instructions followed, which Naomi could obviously neither hear nor follow, but it was clear that Tom was being told in no uncertain terms what he should do with the bag in question. With a final shove of the holdall, Tom's father hurried off, pulling his cap lower on his head so as not to be recognised.

Naomi let out a long breath and was about to step away from the window, when Tom suddenly raised his head from where he had been contemplating the luggage in his lap. Perhaps having felt Naomi's eyes upon him, perhaps just sheer bad luck, she found their gazes suddenly locked.

It was too late to hide, too late to pretend, so Naomi simply turned her back and walked away from the window and into the darker depths of the shop, her heart hammering in her chest. Given their most recent meeting, it was not strange that she didn't wave or otherwise acknowledge him, yet Naomi still had an awful sinking feeling that she'd been caught observing something she shouldn't.

Worried that Tom would come straight over to the café, Naomi hurried into the kitchen and busied herself by beginning the sourdough bread rolls. It was only as the minutes passed by, and there was no jingling of the bell above the door, that the slight tremble in her hands disappeared and she felt herself start to enjoy the familiar process. It was later in the day, when her heart was happy from baking, and her legs tired from standing at the counter, that it dawned on Naomi that she could've just locked the door.

It was just as they were finishing a meal of homemade steak pie with roast potatoes, broccoli and gravy – it turned out Timpson could cook better than Naomi would've expected for a detective who spent so little time at home – that Argyll arrived and asked to speak with Kath again. Naomi saw Sarah's face fall, as her mother-in-law looked around in apparent confusion at the interruption to the evening meal.

"No, no I don't want to go into the living room. You can say what you have to say here, while I finish my dinner," the woman was adamant.

Argyll simply shrugged her shoulders, gave a gesture to the officer with her to keep an eye on the door in case Kath should make a bolt for it, and then sat down at the table beside them all.

Naomi felt extremely awkward, not least because this was a family matter and she was clearly intruding by being there, but also because the thought of Kath trying to do a runner brought an inappropriate snort of laughter that she completely failed to stifle.

"All okay?" Timpson asked her, frowning.

"Yes, yes, sorry, pastry went down the wrong way," Naomi lied, wishing she didn't have such immature coping mechanisms.

"Right then," Argyll began, ignoring the fact that Kath held stubbornly onto her knife and fork and kept playing with her food.

"New information come to light?" Timpson asked, his face a professional mask once more. Had he not taken Sarah's hand in his at that precise moment, it would be easy to think he had just arrived with Argyll to do a job.

"Aye, so, we've returned Mrs. Evans to the manor house."

"Really? That's good news, isn't it?" Naomi couldn't help but speak up.

"Well, it is for Mrs. Evans, yes," Argyll said pointedly, the clear implication being that it wasn't such good news for someone else.

"But she was on the scene, she…" Sarah began, grasping at straws as if she had a feeling what was coming.

"Aye well, the lady says she just drank the tea to steady her nerves after the tragic discovery. It could be a double bluff, of course, to try to trick us, but I dinnae think so," Argyll's strong accent slipped out for a moment, as if she too wasn't so sure but was feeding them the line that had been agreed upon. "I'm not sure that the woman is that bright and conniving, to be honest, nor am I convinced she could strangle a man, looking at how slight she is. Anyway, all circumstantial other than a potential motive regarding a kitten."

Timpson raised his eyebrows, but Argyll didn't elaborate. Naomi, of course, knew exactly what she was referring to.

"So, she's out of the frame, for now anyway," Timpson said slowly, "because you've found…" He waited impatiently for the answer.

"The origin of the sedative," Argyll said, avoiding eye contact with any of them and focusing on Dougal who was hanging around hoping for their leftovers.

After a long, uncomfortable pause, where Kath made a show of continuing obstinately on with her meal, and Sarah looked like she might be sick, the detective's gaze finally landed upon her new top suspect.

"Mrs. Dawson, I believe you take sleeping pills?" Argyll began, as the light of understanding dawned on Timpson's face, telling Naomi all she needed to know about how bad this was about to be for Sarah's mother-in-law.

"I do, and what of it?"

"It has come to our attention, and been verified by your health centre, that the particular brand of sedative found within your sleeping tablets, exactly matches the substance found in the teapot owned by the deceased."

"That means nothing. Maybe he took the same tablets? Or Carys? Or Goldie for that matter!" Kath's voice rose in pitch as she spoke.

"I wondered that too, but checks have proven that's not the case," Argyll remained perfectly calm.

"And I'm not strong enough to kill that fat, lardy man!" Kath added, making her argument seem desperate rather than helping her case.

"You held those fireside tools very well last night," Argyll said, "do you mind if I take them with us to the station? Our investigations have also revealed that there were no open, freshly dug graves at the time of your visit to the cemetery, leaving your claimed alibi quite open for, ah, discussion."

"You're arresting her?" Sarah's voice was half sob as she jumped to her feet.

"Let them do their job, love" Timpson encouraged her to sit back down, "it's just for questioning at the moment."

And so Kath was taken into police custody, and the three of them were left once more with no appetite for either food or conversation.

CHAPTER EIGHTEEN

The next day dawned bleaker than ever, and Naomi was not looking forward to the task which awaited her. Now that Carys was back, she had no choice but to return to Ginger's to drop Bonnie off. It was for the best, of course, because if the two parrots lived together for much longer it would become increasingly hard to separate them. Besides, Reggie needed his big cage brought over here if they were to stay indefinitely at the Salty Sea Dog, which had become Naomi's plan.

Sarah needed help in the Three B's, and Naomi needed to be away from the manor house, for her own mental health if nothing else.

Timpson had kindly offered to take her up there in his car, ostensibly because the cage was too heavy and cumbersome for Naomi to carry back – which it was – but probably with the ulterior motive of having a poke about up there on his own. Either way, Naomi was grateful for the company.

She let them in through the main doors and was about to head straight upstairs to find Carys and return her parrot, when raised voices caught their attention from the end of the corridor.

"Why are there always people arguing around here?" Naomi asked, her feet freezing to the spot of their own accord.

Following behind her, Timpson didn't reply, simply placing a gentle hand on her shoulder to indicate he would go in first. As they entered the ballroom, Naomi put the carrier with Bonnie in it on the nearest round table, and then followed quickly behind the detective, hiding in his shadow.

Standing over by the now redundant grand piano, the two women hadn't noticed their approach, so engrossed were they in their confrontation.

"Docked?" Carys screeched, "Docked? I was being interviewed by the police! You need your head checked, woman! All that heavy jewellery has done you an injury!" Her Welsh accent was so broad in the moment, that Naomi struggled to understand some of the individual words, but the meaning was clear – Carys was furious!

"Obviously I'm not going to pay you for work not done, so your wages will be docked accordingly,"

Goldie replied, looking resplendent in a fuchsia silk kimono, though without her usual lashings of makeup.

"You'll regret that," Carys snarled, just as she caught sight of Timpson approaching from the side and her whole demeanour changed. "Ah, detective, I didn't see you there."

"Evidently," Timpson replied, his tone devoid of any emotion.

Spotting Naomi behind him, Goldie said, "Ah, there you are, girl! Where have you been hiding? Make me some brunch!"

Naomi stood, wide eyed and incredulous, formulating a suitable response that involved telling the woman exactly where she could stick her brunch, when Timpson spoke again, though this time with much more urgency.

"Can anyone smell smoke?"

"Smoke?" Goldie, hands on hips, sniffed the air theatrically.

"Yes, now you come to mention it," Naomi replied.

The four of them looked around the room, and it didn't take long to spot the thin, greyish plumes coming from under the door that led to Goldie's rooms.

"Agh! My baby!" Goldie screamed, launching herself towards that corner of the room, though much impeded by the fluffy, kitten heeled dress slippers she was wearing which caught on the bottom of her kimono and threatened to send her flying.

Timpson reached the door first, covering his nose with his coat and flinging it open. He stood back to allow some of the smoke to escape as the freaked feline launched itself out of the room, landing on Goldie's ample bosom and clinging to the collar of the kimono with no regard for the expensive silk.

"Get off me!" Goldie shrieked, before remembering herself and adding, "My gorgeous Ginger. Thank goodness you're safe."

Timpson grabbed one of the fire extinguishers which the fire department had insisted be installed throughout the building during the renovation in order to sign off the manor house's fire certificate, and walked into the smoke-filled room.

"Call the fire brigade!" Naomi shouted at Carys, who was frozen behind them, before following the detective into the burning room.

A few strong blasts on the extinguisher later, and the fire had thankfully been stopped in its tracks.

"It was just the curtain, went up fast due to the combustible nature of the synthetic fibres, I think, but we'll have to have it tested to see if an accelerant was used," Timpson said, matter-of-factly, then more softly, "Naomi, you shouldn't have followed me in here. We didn't know what we were going to find."

"Sarah would kill me if I let anything happen to you," Naomi said, earning her a quick grin.

"Ah, I've been in much worse situations than this," Timpson joked, "though that cat is pretty scary!"

Naomi couldn't help a snort, the humour helping her anxiety, as Timpson opened the patio doors in Goldie's quarters. Naomi hadn't realised her employer had these in her room too, guessing they'd always been hidden behind the curtains, and that Goldie could therefore go out of the back of the building whenever she wanted and return without being seen.

"Now, the big question is, was this an accident?" The detective asked the ladies as they all stood outside on the rear path oft used by Naomi and others. "Certainly, if I hadn't been here things would've escalated pretty quickly. It could've been much worse."

Goldie held her head dramatically, complaining of smoke inhalation, despite her having not breathed in anything of the such and now being stood in the fresh air, whilst Carys remained sour-faced and silent off to the side. Ginger, having seen her chance and taken it, had scarpered off to the bottom of the garden without Goldie noticing, a sweet escape indeed.

It was then that it hit Naomi that what had just occurred was a fire. A fire in the manor house, just as Tom's father had threatened.

She felt her legs wobble as the realisation hit her, wondering why it hadn't been her first thought despite the urgency of the moment.

"Are you okay, Naomi? Let me get you a seat and some water," Timpson's face was etched in worry.

"I, ah, I think there's something you should know," Naomi said, before the world went black.

CHAPTER NINETEEN

"Now, fainting is Goldie's trick" Carys said as she held a cold cloth to Naomi's brow.

"So, about the fire," Timpson had been a true gentleman, catching Naomi and carrying her to a wooden bench further down the garden, but he was also clearly impatient to get the details Naomi had remembered.

Goldie was back inside, flirting with the firefighters and asking them to repeatedly check her pulse, so the detective suggested Carys might want to go and save them so that the poor people could actually get on with their job and find out if the fire was accidental or not.

Naomi was pretty sure she knew the answer to that already and told him so as soon as the housekeeper was out of sight.

"Why wasn't this reported, Naomi?" Timpson's voice was gentle, but his tone frustrated, as he ran a hand through his damp hair. "Or even just mentioned quietly to me? I could've made some enquiries."

"At first, the incident with Kath and Colin and then his murder took precedence, and to be honest Mr. Hornsley's threats slipped my mind. I didn't deliberately withhold the information. But then Tom…" She trailed off, reliving Tom's angry, aggressive behaviour in her mind.

"It's okay, Naomi, I know it's hard. It's been a lot to deal with, in such a short space of time. For all of us –

even me, and I'm a pro," Timpson waited patiently then, his eyes encouraging her to speak.

"Well, Tom told me in no uncertain terms not to tell the police about his father's visit."

"Did he threaten you?" Timpson probed gently.

"He, he…" the tears began, and Naomi could no longer bottle them up.

"Okay, it's okay, we can talk about that later if you like. Just tell me, do you think either Tom or his father could have set this place alight?"

"Yes, I do, from what I know of Tom he's only staying here to please his dad, to dig up dirt on Goldie for the inheritance opposition case. Now that those legal channels have failed, I guess they're getting desperate," Naomi whispered, suddenly remembering the scene with that same pair yesterday, and the transfer of the holdall and telling Timpson about it.

"A brown leather holdall, you say?" Timpson clarified.

"Yes, a battered looking one."

Right, well you stay here, and I'll just have a quiet look around," he stood, casting a searching gaze around the garden.

"No! I'll come," Naomi really didn't want to be left alone in this place right now.
"Okay, but stay close."

They took the outside route back around to the front of the building, deliberately avoiding being seen by Carys or Goldie, and re-entered through the main doors.

"We'll try Tom's room first," Timpson whispered, leading the way up the stairs.

Naomi felt her heartrate rise as he knocked on her neighbour's door.

"Best to check first," the detective whispered.

Thankfully there was no reply and Timpson simply let himself in, doing a quick scan of the room as Naomi hovered in the doorway, unsure of what to do. The detective looked quickly in the wardrobe and under the bed, finding nothing of note, and within minutes they were doing the same in the upstairs kitchen.

"Probably too obvious," Timpson said, leading them back downstairs, though this time turning left instead of right, and starting down the unrenovated corridor which led to the partially dilapidated conservatory.

"As I recall, this was where we found the rat poison," the detective said as he lifted dust covers and looked under rotting rattan furniture.

"Bingo!" He exclaimed, pulling a brown bag – now covered in dust and spiders' webs from being shoved under an ancient bamboo settee – out into the open. "I guess he thought we'd presume lightening doesn't strike twice in the same spot, but believe me, in this line of work you learn not to assume anything."

The bag was empty, which Naomi had to admit was rather anti-climactic, but Timpson wasn't discouraged. With the evidence secured and now wrapped in a once-white, now greying cotton sheet, he rushed back to the front doors, out of the building, and round towards the gardener's cottage.

Naomi hurried to keep up with him, likening it to following a dog who had caught a scent and could do nothing but impulsively follow it. In a matter of minutes they had reached Colin's cottage, the police tape still stuck across the door.

"Well, since I am the police..." Timpson said confidently as he dipped under it and opened the door with ease. Clearly, it had remained unlocked since the murder. Naomi followed suit, noticing that the plastic 'do not cross' tape looked untouched as she did so.

How many people could've just done this? And there'd be no sign of entry? She wondered.

The place was dim in the dullness of the day, with the curtains only partially opened. Naomi felt like she was intruding, invading Colin's space, but Timpson forged ahead, clearly this was par for the course in his line of work. The detective passed Naomi the grubby parcel containing the bag, and no sooner had he started looking than he found an empty petrol can shoved behind a tall floor lamp.

"How did you know?" Naomi whispered, "That it would be here?"

"A hunch," Timpson replied, "and the most logical place to dump something if you're disturbed setting a fire and need to offload it somewhere at the back of the building. This is the place you'd assume no one would check now that the forensics team have finished. Quite clever, really…"

"…But not clever enough," Naomi finished for him.

Timpson grinned, then began a search of the rest of the room as Naomi started to wonder what would happen when the arsonist came back to get rid of the evidence and found it missing.

Given that the top two suspects were known to resort to aggression, she certainly didn't want to be around when that happened.

How did I not see it? She chided herself, a chill running through her as the unheated stone cottage was far too cold to linger long in. *How did I not see there were so many red flags I could've made bunting from them?*

"These things aren't always obvious, people can be chameleons, or perhaps our self-defence mechanisms don't always kick in to allow us to see them. Sometimes we see what we want to see," Timpson replied, and Naomi realised she'd spoken her thoughts out loud.

A warm blush spread up her cheeks and she was glad when the detective said they'd call it a day for now and let the fire officer write up his report whilst the police could do another proper search of the place.

"I'll call this in from the car and we can drop the evidence with Argyll on the way home," the detective said, clearly pleased with his haul.

"But isn't the fire separate from the murder case?" Naomi asked.

"It is, and it isn't. Same location, same suspects potentially. Who knows who's in cahoots? Mrs. Evans seemed particularly angry today."

"Umhm," Naomi mulled it over, only realising as they drove away that in all the apparent excitement she had completely forgotten to collect Reggie's cage.

CHAPTER TWENTY

Argyll met them in the police station car park, her coat flapping open in the wind and giving the impression of her having bat wings. Naomi managed a smile at the image and wound down her window to say hello, whilst Timpson got out of the car to talk to his colleague.

"Are you certain, though?" Naomi heard Timpson ask in hushed tones.

"I learnt from the best," Argyll replied, "she's got Motive – a strong one too, since she believes he caused her son's death – Method, with the crushed sleeping tablets she had right to hand, and Means, she was missing for several hours and the town CCTV has clocked her on the coastal path behind the manor house at the approximate time of death. Tick, tick, tick, just like you taught me."

"Hmm," Timpson sounded unconvinced.

"Look, I know you have a personal connection here, but how many times have relatives told us it just can't possibly be true? That their loved one couldn't be a killer. I mean, there was the violent outburst the night before, which could have led to a much worse outcome if we hadn't intervened."

"I know, I know," Timpson scraped a hand across his face, "and there were no security cameras at the cemetery?"

"None that were working. They've got them up at the main gate, but I'd hazard a guess they've been out of action for a long while, we did ask of course. The cameras on the promenade don't cover the back gate to the manor house directly, so she could easily have slipped in that way unnoticed."

"With that hulking dog?" Timpson asked, clearly trying to cover all bases.

"Who knows? Perhaps he stayed on the path or on the beach? Does it matter, so long as it doesn't change the fundamentals?"

"What about the private investigator?"

"No luck finding him, probably made himself scarce with the money."

"The sedative could've been bought online, stolen…" Timpson clutched at every straw.

"The boxes are ticked. We've made the arrest, I'm sorry mate," Argyll shook her head.

"Well, get forensics onto these, will you? There's more going on up there, I'm sure of it. And keep me updated." Timpson handed her the wrapped bag and fuel can and returned to the car, restless and disheartened. He tapped his fingers several times against the steering wheel before starting the engine.

"You don't agree with the decision to officially arrest Kath?" Naomi ventured to ask.

The detective paused before replying, evidently collecting his thoughts, "Argyll is right about the Motive, Method and Means, and ordinarily I'd write it up as a job well done, but something about this one doesn't sit right with me."

"Because it's Kath?"

"Yes and no. Yes, because I've gotten to know her these past couple of months, and of course Sarah knows her very well, and we both agree Kath just isn't the violent type. The other night was extremely out of character for her, but I guess that's often the case for murders too – people get carried away." He sighed heavily.

"And no?"

"Well, that's because even when I think about it logically, force myself to be impartial, I still feel dissatisfied by this outcome."

"You have doubts?" Naomi asked.

"I do. There are just too many loose threads, too many possible suspects and unexplored avenues," Timpson shook his head.

"So, what will you do?" Naomi wondered.

"Well, I can't rest with Kath in jail, not that Sarah would let me anyway," he gave a wry smile that didn't reach his eyes, "and my own ethics won't let me end an investigation until I'm sure we have the right person, so…"

"So, you're going to keep searching for evidence?"

"Within my current limited means, yes. I'm back at work tomorrow, onto the next case, but in my spare time… well, we'll see."

They lapsed into silence then, with Naomi thinking that Kath was very lucky to have such a fair man in her corner. But then Timpson himself had been taught by the best, her dad, Adam Bramble, and his former colleague, Detective McArthur.

What would Dad make of all this? Naomi wondered, the homesickness hitting hard once again.

Whether it was the universe manifesting her unspoken wishes, or a higher entity hearing her prayers, Naomi didn't know, but the text message that she received that evening brought a strength of relief even she hadn't expected.

"Dad? I got you message," Naomi phoned him straight back.

"Aye love, we've just got home, so I can come and collect the feathered overlord in the morning, if that's okay?"

"That would be perfect," Naomi felt her chest release a deep breath, "we'll be ready!"

CHAPTER TWENTY-ONE

Of course, it had barely changed.

She had been away for less than a year, after all.

Despite the heavy drizzle, Naomi wound down her passenger side window and took in all the familiar sights – the old church sitting at the top of the village green, the cottage on Front Street where Granny Betty and Grandad Harry had lived, the shops with their punny names, and the Bun in the Oven pub on the corner.

As they rounded the corner onto the driveway which led to the tearoom and further on to her home at The Rise, Naomi felt a tear track down her cheek, an outward sign of her inner release. Release of worry and tension, release of stress and insecurity.

She was home.

"My Flora!" Reggie screeched, the moment he was released into the Tearoom on the Rise.

"Yes, I'm back, no doubt you'll be scamming me out of lots of fruit to make up for leaving you," Flora focused on the bird, until she caught sight of her daughter exiting the car behind.

"Naomi? I wasn't expecting to see you too! What a perfect surprise!"

"Hi Mum," Naomi walked into the outstretched arms that had been her constant safe space over the past decade, the place of no judgement or expectation, and breathed in the smell of home.

"Overcooked the scones again?" She joked, to hide her emotion.

"Well, you know me, I get distracted," Flora replied, stepping back slightly to take in the measure of her daughter. "You look tired, love, Tanya will be here soon to take over and we can head up to the house for a catch up. How long can you stay?"

Naomi caught her dad giving a quick shake of his head, which prompted Flora to add, "Back for a while, I hope."

"I left most of my stuff there, just brought the things I had at the pub with me, so I'll have to go back at some point," Naomi was trying not to dwell on that fact.

"No need to worry, we'll get that sorted. You've plenty of gear at home to keep you going. And Mr. Reginald here, with his perch in every place, won't go without," Adam joked.

"Thank you," Naomi whispered, grateful to not have to explain straight away.

"My No Me! My Flora!" Reggie flew around in excited contentment, delighted to have his two favourites back together in one place, "She's a corker!"

Thank you so much for following Naomi's story so far! Don't worry, she and Reggie will be back in Bakerslea-by-the-Sea very soon for the final instalment of the murder mystery there, and they won't be arriving alone!

Look out for some sleuthing help, too, as Adam is reunited with his protégé and the real detective work begins!

"Fake it Till You Cake It!"

Coming Soon

Have you visited Baker's Rise, where it all began?

Read "Here Today, Scone Tomorrow," and see how Reggie came flying into Flora's life!

ABOUT THE AUTHOR

Rachel Hutchins lives in northeast England with her husband, three children and their dog Boudicca. She loves writing both mysteries and romances, and enjoys reading these genres too! Her favourite place is walking along the local coastline, with a coffee and some cake!

You can connect with via her website at: www.authorrachelhutchins.com

Alternatively, she has social media pages on:

Facebook: www.facebook.com/rahutchinsauthor

Instagram: www.instagram.com/ra_hutchins_author

Printed in Dunstable, United Kingdom